to Ginell—

MOON CRUSHER

SUSAN KITE

Susan Kite
2021

This is a work of fiction. Names, characters, places, and incidents are products of the author's imagination or are used fictitiously and are not to be construed as real. Any resemblance to actual events, locations, organizations, or persons, living or dead, is entirely coincidental.

World Castle Publishing, LLC
Pensacola, Florida
Copyright © Susan Kite 2020
Paperback ISBN: 9781951642686
eBook ISBN: 9781951642693
First Edition World Castle Publishing, LLC, May 25, 2020
http://www.worldcastlepublishing.com
Licensing Notes
All rights reserved. No part of this book may be used or reproduced in any manner whatsoever without written permission, except in the case of brief quotations embodied in articles and reviews.
Cover: Karen Fuller
Editor: Maxine Bringenberg

Prologue

Commander Diego Perez of the Velossian sector of the Seressin Empire had finally made it back to the home he'd felt he would never see again. He left his apprentice behind as he entered the small church. Left behind also were the emblems of his rank and power. They had no meaning in this place. Diego carried a dirk inside his armor and a hand laser inside his sleeve. He wore his dark military uniform, but it was devoid of decoration and badges.

Of the huge wooden doors that had once fascinated him with their ornate carvings of painted birds and saints, only one was left, and it was hanging askew by one hinge. A live bird exploded in a flurry of feathers and squawking indignation above his head as he walked into the church. The full moon shone through a large hole in the ceiling. This was the church where he had gone to mass with his family. It had been vibrant, busy, and alive when he had been here last. How long ago? Barely ten years? How could this have happened in so short a time? And what had happened? It was inconceivable that there would be no church for those who lived nearby.

Leaves and other debris crunched under his feet as he walked toward the balustrade and the altar. The moonlight showed ghosts of the bright paint that had covered the walls. Birds roosted where the statuary once stood. Other creatures rustled in the shadows of the walls.

Diego approached the bare and weather-beaten altar and genuflected. Before he got up, he prayed that he might be able to find out what had happened here. Anaar had told him that space travel distorted time, but still, there should have been something, someone. The soft sigh of the wind outside was all he heard. He got up and turned back toward the door.

"Who are you?" a low voice asked from the doorway where the priests used to enter to perform mass.

"I am Commander Diego Perez y Andres Morales. And who are you?" he asked the shadow.

"I am Bernardo Fortuna."

"What happened here?"

"Ah, you have been away. Your family name is familiar. Are you related to Don Reynaldo Perez? They owned much land around here for many years."

"Yes. Don Reynaldo is my brother. And I have been away; far away."

"Ah, the son who disappeared under strange and frightening conditions. I am sorry to bear you the sad news that your brother, señor, no longer lives. He died almost ten years ago. His daughter and son-in-law take care of what is left of the rancho."

Ten years?! How long had he been gone, in terms of years

on Earth? "What year is it, Señor Fortuna?"

"What a strange question. It would be the same year in South America, or anywhere else, as it is here."

"I have been far into the frontier." That was technically true, although this man's brain would never understand how far a frontier it was.

"It is 1849, my friend."

More than twenty years. He had lived ten to Earth's twenty. "What happened here?"

"First the corrupt administrados, and then war with the Americanos. The Americans have pretty much taken over everything, including the land. Your family was lucky to have saved even a small portion of the large hacienda your father once owned."

"So the Mexican government won independence and then couldn't hold on to their lands," Diego conjectured.

"That is about it, señor. Since the Spanish priests went away, the missions have suffered."

There was little he could do about it. "Thank you for your information to a tired traveler. Let me reward you." Diego pulled out a gold nugget and handed it to the man, who had barely stepped out of the shadows.

The man scuttled forward and took the proffered gift. "Is this gold? I have heard of this farther north, but not here. Gracias, señor, gracias!"

Diego decided to take a chance. "Can I trust you to take something to my brother's family?"

"Of course, of course."

Diego hastily wrote a short note on paper he had brought with him. He folded it and put it in a small packet. "Good.

Here is a letter addressed to my niece. Give this to her. Here is more gold for your efforts." Diego handed him a small pouch of gold dust.

The man's eyes nearly popped out of their sockets when he looked inside. "Holy Mother of God watch over and bless you! I will take this immediately!"

"Thank you, Señor Fortuna!"

"*De nada*, amigo. Go in peace."

After the old man left, Diego walked behind the altar and pulled out the litter that had collected. He found a place where another bag of nuggets would be hidden from all except one who knew exactly where to look. Once the gold was hidden, he replaced the rubbish. He strode out of the church and gazed at the moonlit countryside. Diego remembered the last time he stood on this land. It was now a land that was alien to him. He remembered his capture and those first days in a place that had been so horrifying to him….

Chapter One

Oh, please, go away! Leave me alone! Holy Mother of God, help me! Diego's mind cried as the soft footfalls came closer. "Santa Maria!" he moaned out loud. His fear was like a fire consuming dry tinder, threatening to overwhelm him.

How long had he been here? He had been riding his horse, Tejas, in the hills, trying to find an answer to his anger. He had not seen the green of the new growth on the hills of his father's rancho. He didn't hear the crows cawing their alarm, didn't hear the out of place wheezing, whistling, and clanking noises until it was too late. His mind was replaying his father announcing his intention to give Reynaldo complete control over the rancho, the thousands of acres of land, the innumerable head of cattle and horses, and the hillsides of grapes. Everything!

He, Diego, the fourteen-year-old son of Miguel Francisco Morales, would be left with nothing in a few short years. Not even the horse he was riding, his beloved Tejas, the gelding he had raised from a colt, would be his because it all belonged to his brother now.

Then Diego had heard the strange noises, had seen the horrible demon-like creatures. They killed Tejas with a weapon that shot fire. When he jumped off his dying horse's back to run, they had caught him. One with scales like a snake grabbed him by one arm. Another with grey fur and yellow cat eyes grabbed the other arm. Another snake demon snatched the front of his shirt and tore his hat off his head, almost decapitating him when the leather string didn't immediately give. That demon was larger than the others. He jerked Diego toward him. The boy remembered the foulness of the demon's breath, the horrid redness of its lidless eyes. He remembered gagging, wanting to throw up his breakfast. Still, he had struggled. Was this his punishment from God for being angry with his brother, for cursing him? The demon pulled back his arm, and Diego saw a taloned fist coming toward his face. Everything went black.

***

The footsteps stopped. He heard whispery breathing and then felt the light touch of a velvet-skinned hand. Diego cried out again, trying to press closer to the cold metal wall. He pulled his arms tighter around his head, trying to shut out everything in this hellish place. The room he had awakened in was bare and stark. The air whooshed sibilantly around him. Where was the sky, where was the warm dusty earth, the smell of junipers after a spring rain?

Right now, Diego didn't care if he was the youngest son of the richest rancher near San Gabriel in Mexican California, maybe fit to inherit a few acres of land, some scrawny cattle, and swaybacked horses at the whim of his haughty brother.

He didn't care; he wanted to go home. To be free of this hellish purgatory.

"Skrekorismmm," a voice said, breaking into his misery. It was a soft voice, with an almost musical cadence.

No! Leave me alone!

My son, he heard his father speaking in the deep recesses of his mind. *My son, be brave. Take what you have. Build on it. It is more than your grandfather had. If you work hard, you will win in life.* It had been small comfort then after his father gave everything to his oldest brother, but he saw the wisdom of it now. If he was in purgatory, he would take his punishment, and then he would see the Virgin, be rescued by her. If these creatures were not from hell…well, he wasn't sure what he would do, but he couldn't sit in the corner forever. *Be brave, be brave,* the voice continued to say to the beat of his heart.

"Krisorinmo?" the voice asked. Diego felt the touch again, and he shivered.

Be brave!

***

Diego remembered not too long ago when he was out with his father's vaqueros. The bright stars twinkling above him, he felt the coolness of the evening breezes and heard the crackling of their fire. There was a howling nearby. "Coyote," he had said.

"No, it is el lobo, the wolf," Miguel said. "We must be vigilant. They will be after the new foals and calves."

Diego remembered riding with Roberto a short time later around the perimeter of the camp. "Something does not feel right," the vaquero murmured.

Then it happened. A twig snapped, and a form flew toward

them, knocking Roberto to the ground. The wolf snapped and growled, reaching for Roberto's throat. The vaquero beat at the animal's head with one hand while trying to get a hold of the wolf's neck with the other.

Diego leaped from his horse while drawing his pistol, trying to aim at the maddened creature.

"Shoot, Diego, shoot!" Roberto cried.

Trying to locate the fallen man in the darkness by his voice, the boy aimed at the growls. He fired, and heard a yelp and then more growls. Diego pulled out his knife and got into a crouch, waiting. "Roberto?" he called. In the dim moonlight, Diego saw the yellow eyes of the wolf as it began creeping toward him. It turned its head and snapped at something, then resumed stalking Diego. "Roberto?"

The wolf crouched, preparing to spring. Diego threw his useless pistol at the animal and held his knife in front of him. The wolf sprang. Diego jerked to one side, raking the blade across the animal's ribs. He felt the wind of the wolf's passing. He heard a pistol shot from behind him and pivoted. Several vaqueros had pistols and muskets ready.

They weren't needed. The wolf lay in a heap, its back legs twitching in death. Then it was still. Miguel walked over to the animal and examined it, holding a burning limb close. Diego rushed to Roberto's side. The vaquero still lay on the ground.

"Roberto." Diego stared in horror at the blood staining the man's chest, pouring from his throat.

Roberto gasped for breath. "You were brave, very brave, my friend," he whispered, then coughed. "Watch for rabid wolves among men."

Diego grabbed the dying man's hand and held it tightly. Roberto had taught him to ride, rope, and shoot. They had spent many hours talking together. Roberto was more of a brother than his own brother had been. His heart squeezed tight and then expanded until he thought he would choke. Diego felt tears prickling in the corners of his eyes and blinked to get rid of them. Men didn't cry, his father had told him.

"Diego, do not expect anything from others. Make your own future." More gasping, more blood, and then with a sigh, Roberto was dead.

Diego held the dead man's hand for a few more minutes, wishing there was some way to bring Roberto back. Any way....

***

The touch on his hand was gentle, and Diego opened his eyes. The demon in front of him had round eyes that were as blue as robin's eggs and as lustrous as pearls. A lavender down covered his body. Diego remembered this one. He had come with a bowl of something that resembled green porridge. It had been left, untouched, by the door where it was placed. The creature didn't remain last time; it pulled out the uneaten food and slid in a fresh bowl, standing in the doorway and gazing at him for a moment before leaving.

This time, though, the creature stayed and then approached. It was small, the top of its head reaching below Diego's waist. Its fingers were short and pudgy. Its ears were small bumps on each side of its head, while the nose was a nubbin above a mouth that resembled a fish's. It held out the new bowl, the contents steaming. Diego's stomach growled, but he made no move to take the demon's offering.

"Phris," the lavender creature said, pointing to himself.

Diego continued to gaze at the little beast, not moving. Despite his fear, he looked into the little man's bluish eyes and felt its kindness.

It pointed at the bowl and made motions of eating what was inside. "Krylis," it said, the round mouth elongating into a thin line.

Diego wasn't sure if it was trying to smile or grimace, but he assumed it was the former. The creature held the bowl closer to Diego.

"Krylis," it repeated.

Diego leaned forward and gazed into the bowl. There were various things inside, some that looked like twigs and some bits that resembled variegated leaves. At the bottom of the bowl was a lump of reddish paste.

The creature picked up one of the sticks and stuck it in the paste. Then it handed the stick to Diego. There was something about this being that reassured Diego. He took the stick, studied it, and then nibbled the end with the paste.

The little man put the bowl down, puffed his cheeks, and clapped his hands together. Then he sat back on his haunches and watched as Diego chewed and swallowed.

The paste had a slightly tart flavor, like that of oranges before full ripeness. The stick was sweet, almost like the taste of sugar cane his uncle Juan had once brought from Cuba. Diego continued nibbling on the stick until he suddenly found it gone. The fuzzy creature puffed his cheeks again and held out the bowl. Diego took it and quickly ate the remaining sticks. He bit into one of the leaf things and found it was good, too. His stomach was still growling as he swallowed the last bite. Residual paste sat in the bottom of the bowl. Diego used his finger to scrape the bowl, savoring the last bite.

He held out the bowl and smiled. The lavender creature cocked his head and stared at Diego's mouth. Diego smiled again, inclined his head, and said, "Gracias, señor."

"Smophix?" the creature said, pointing one stubby finger at Diego's face.

Diego shook his head, not understanding. He did point inside the empty bowl making motions of eating more food.

The creature's eyes looked sad, and then he made a motion with his fingers. "Kras," was all he said, but Diego assumed he was being told no.

With a sigh, Diego handed the bowl back and leaned against the wall. The lavender furred creature touched him on the shoulder and then pointed to itself. "Phris," it said. It pointed again. "Phris."

Could that be its name, Diego wondered? Then krylis must have been the name of the food. He pointed at the little man. "Phris?"

Eyes sparkling, the creature made a huffing sound, clearly pleased.

Diego pointed to himself. "Diego."

Phris touched him on the chest. "Dee-a-ya-go," he said.

Diego smiled and nodded, pointing to himself. "Diego." Then he pointed to Phris. "Phris."

Phris reached over with one stubby hand and tugged on his shirt, pointing to the door. Did he want Diego to leave? Maybe Phris was going to take him home. Getting up, Diego followed the strange creature. The lavender man held his hand up to a red spot on the wall by the door and waited.

There was a beep, and the door slid open like a curtain. Diego peered at it, but at a sound and gesture from Phris, he walked out of the little room.

He followed Phris down hallways that were of the same cold metal as his cell, gray and drab. There was light, but no lanterns or candles. Diego gazed upward at the ceiling, wondering how this could be. There was no window to let sunlight in either. They turned a corner, and Diego saw another plain hallway. They did this several more times, and he wondered how Phris could find his way around.

Phris stopped at the end of the corridor and put his hand on another spot like the one that had been in the other room. Another door slid open, and Diego gazed into a tiny room. Phris motioned him in, but Diego balked, imagining himself locked in this room not much bigger than a confessional. Shaking his head, he backed up. Phris gazed at him, then walked into the little room. With soft sounds and more gestures, the little creature beckoned to him. Diego stepped in and heard the door close behind him.

Suddenly, the young man felt the floor shudder, and the room acted as though it were moving. Earthquake, he asked himself? Diego stared wildly at Phris. The lavender creature made his soothing sounds and touched him lightly on the arm. It was reassuring, but Diego's heart still beat wildly.

After a short while, the movement ended, and the door opened again, this time to a larger room. Diego stared in open-mouthed wonder. How could he go into this little room from a hallway and end up in a large room, he wondered? On one side of the room were several of the creatures like those who had captured him. His fear began to grow again, filling his chest with dread.

The scaled demon made motions with his clawed fingers, and Phris moved forward, pulling at Diego's sleeve when the young man balked. The dark, olive-green demon's speech was like the barking and growling of coyotes mixed with the hissing of snakes. It was stridently loud, hurting his ears. Diego shuffled as close as Phris made him.

The demon shot out a reptilian arm and hooked its claws into his already tattered shirt. His trousers were not in much better shape, the cuffs shredded. The dirty fabric ripped, but the boy still ended up face to face with this monster from hell. His eyes wide with fear, Diego tried to turn his head enough to avoid the horror's fetid breath. He gagged.

With a growl, the demon jerked his head back toward him, roaring. Diego felt blood trickle down his cheek from the creature's claws. It grabbed his hair and jerked his face even closer. The pain brought tears to the corners of his eyes, but Diego would not cry out. That resolution was short-lived. The demon let go of his shirt and back-handed him across the face. It did this twice before releasing his hair.

Diego flew across the room and landed hard on the metal floor. He lay there a few seconds before sitting up. Swiping his hand across his eyes, Diego slowly climbed to his knees. Phris was gesturing to the demon. The scaled creature slapped Phris across the room, too. The lavender man hit the wall and lay motionless. Diego rose to his feet, his eyes never leaving the demon. The creature turned to him, growled ferociously, and then left, his fellow demons following. They all barked and slapped their thighs. Diego could have sworn they were laughing.

Anger replaced his fear, and the boy dashed over to his companion. Phris was slowly coming around, making little hooting noises and holding his head. Diego gestured, trying to find out if Phris was injured. The lavender creature pointed to his head, and the boy touched the place, feeling a lump above one ear. The lavender man wrapped a hand around Diego's wrist and motioned a desire for the boy's help. Diego grasped Phris's hand and pulled. The down-covered man was heavier than he looked, and Diego doubled his efforts.

When he was on his feet, Phris leaned against the wall for a moment, rubbing his head. Then he gestured to Diego, something that told him Phris was pleased. It was frustrating not being able to communicate with his new friend. All he could do was smile or frown. He smiled, happy that his strange friend wasn't hurt.

Phris motioned for Diego to follow him. Looking around, the boy saw no other demons or any other large creatures that might hurt them. With a shrug, he followed Phris to the opposite wall where two different creatures leaned against a huge opening, something akin to a window. They were scaled like the big demon, but their scales were smaller and a bright orange. Each man-shaped demon had a bony red crest on its head. Phris hooted, and one of the creatures turned away, walking among racks of what appeared to be clothes.

Diego gazed at its companion, who waited at the window. Both of them were thin, almost skeletal, their limbs stick-like. The eyes were small, dark-green, and beady above a nose that was a vertical slit. The mouth was a horizontal slash, lipless and wide.

It stared back at him and then shoved him away from the

window. Angered, Diego slapped at the stick hand and, with a growl, stalked back to the window. He was tired of being pushed around. They may be demons, but if he was in Hell, at least he was going to act like a *hacendado*'s son who still had his honor.

Diego remembered that one did not gain respect with the vaqueros by backing away from a contest or worrying about the danger. The face drew close to his, and the mouth, filled with sharp pointed teeth, opened in a grimace. A sudden spear of panic shot through his body, but Diego stood his ground, staring into the beady eyes.

Again the hand shot out, but this time Diego grabbed it. The fingers even felt like twigs, and the boy expected them to break in his grasp. With his other hand, Diego shoved the creature away from him while letting go of the stick man's hand. Surprised, the scaled stick-demon fell backward to the ground, clattering in a heap. The thin mouth opened wide in surprise, and the dark eyes scrutinized him closely. Finally, he rose from the floor, and with a lingering look, followed the other stick man to the back of the room.

Chapter Two

Phris touched him on the arm, and Diego turned to see the lavender man staring at him, his blue eyes sparkling with humor. His mouth was a round oh, and the creature's soft hooting was like laughter, celebrating this little triumph. Phris then made a motion that Diego thought might be a warning to be careful when the stick-men returned. He nodded and turned when he heard the twig creatures. The first one threw two garments onto the counter and pointed to him. Phris motioned for Diego to pick them up. The little man tugged at his torn and dirty clothes and gestured for him to change into the new suit. Looking around, the boy wondered if he was supposed to change in front of these creatures.

Phris cocked his head and pointed toward a nearby door. Again Diego nodded and followed the little man into the other room. It was small and bare, except for a bench. The boy peeled off the torn shirt, the frayed pants, and then held up the new suit. The shirt and pants were connected, making it all one piece. Diego wondered how to open it up to put it on. Phris saw his dilemma and took it from him. He made a motion with his hands on part of the fabric, and the top of the suit opened down the front, almost to the legs.

Phris handed him another piece of clothing. Diego recognized what it was immediately — underwear. Blushing slightly, he turned away from Phris and pulled off his grimy undergarments. The new one was one piece, much like the one he had taken off. Again there were no buttons or hooks. He tried to imitate the motion Phris had made, but the clothing didn't open for him. He tried again, his hand brushing the material. This time the opening appeared. It seemed magical.

Diego slipped on the garment and marveled at its softness. This was much better than the wool he was used to. Diego wondered how to close the opening. Again Phris came to the rescue, this time running his hand in the opposite direction. The material fastened together, barely showing a seam. Diego put on the suit and followed the same motion the little man had done with the underwear. It worked! Amazed, Diego tugged at the material, which held together unless he touched the top. Touching the top again, it slid open with ease. Satisfied, Diego closed the opening and then ran his hand down the sides of his suit. It was every bit as comfortable as the undergarment.

Phris tugged at his sleeve and pointed toward the door. Diego started to gather his old clothes. As dirty as they were, they were still the only thing he had left of home. The lavender-downed man motioned for him to leave them. The boy assumed the servants would take care of them, but would he get them back? Figuring he wouldn't, Diego picked up his once-fancy trousers that his mother had decorated with beadwork, unable to leave that remnant of home. He glanced at the door where Phris was waiting and saw the little man's eyes examining him. The creature hooted and made a motion that Diego assumed was one of approval.

Phris led him down several other corridors and into another small moving room. It traveled for a short while and then opened into a corridor identical to the others Diego had been in so far. They went down this hallway and through a doorway to a room with strange furnishings. There were many tables, bare of ornamentation, but each one held things that whirred and clicked. Some of these things had pictures that moved and sang.

Diego stood in the doorway, transfixed. Phris patted his arm and motioned him to one of the tables. Slowly, the boy followed him. The little man sat down on a bench in front of a table and pointed for Diego to sit next to him. Shoving away his anxiety over the strange devices, he did as asked and faced the moving pictures with Phris.

Objects floated and whisked across the front of the rectangular box like fireflies being chased on humid summer nights near the lake. Diego peered behind the box but could see no place where the tiny objects could have gotten in. Phris made his hooting/laughing sound and handed him something that slightly resembled a hat with no brim. There were flaps that covered his ears.

Diego studied it, frowning, and then looked at Phris, wondering what he was supposed to do with it. Gently, Phris took it from him, stood up, and placed it on his head. Then his companion pointed toward the box. Staring at it, Diego was shocked to see the picture changing, and was even more shocked to hear sounds coming from the hat that covered his ears. He reached up to tear it off his head, but Phris firmly held his hand and motioned that the hat was safe. Diego wasn't as sure, but he lowered his hand, listened to the voice, and watched the pictures.

The voice was low but somewhat raspy. He was unable to understand the words, but as he watched the pictures on the box, he began to understand that the voice was telling him what the picture on the box was. It kept saying the same thing over and over again as it showed the same picture, one of the large lizard-men. Listening to the same word over and over again, Diego finally repeated it. "Seressin." The box showed bright, flashing colors, and the hat made soothing, pleasant sounds. Diego assumed the hat and box were pleased with him. Could the hat and the box be like some kind of teacher? Like the priest who had taught him to read and write? Surely this was impossible. No teacher other than Father Guiseppe had made pleasant sounds when they were teaching him. How could a box do the same things a human teacher did? This was of the devil. Diego snatched the hat off.

Phris shook his head and took the hat from Diego's hand. He put it on his own head, hooting something in a soothing tone.

Diego knew Phris was trying to reassure him. He took the hat and put it back on. The picture came on the box again without the hat saying anything. After a while, the word sounded in his ears, and Diego repeated it. "Seressin." More pleasant sounds, more soothing colors. The hat did this several more times before going on to another picture and sound. Diego relaxed and tried to enjoy this strange teaching experience.

After a great deal of time, Diego took off the teaching hat and looked at Phris. "You are Hoorinoo?" he asked, pointing at the lavender-colored figure on the screen.

Phris gave the new language word for yes, hooting with pleasure at Diego's progress. "You (garbled word) fast."

Diego assumed the unknown word was *learn*. "I do not like...um...no talking," he answered. It was true. He remembered Father saying once that his eager mouth sometimes passed his brain. He remembered all the long talks with Miguel, talks he would never have again. Diego felt a tightening in his chest as he thought about his home on the hacienda. Sister, brother, mother, father. He squeezed his eyes shut so tears wouldn't form.

"We will do...learning tomorrow," Phris said, his hand lightly touching Diego's shoulder.

After five day-cycles, Diego felt he could at least make himself understood and understand others as well. He had spent most of the days in the learning room with the teaching helmet — headphones and computer, as he learned the box with pictures was called.

His sleep time was spent in a tiny room he shared with Phris. When they weren't sleeping, Diego practiced talking the Seressin tongue with Phris. He tried to coax the lavender alien into teaching him some of his own language, or for Diego to teach the Hoorinoo Spanish, but Phris resisted. Diego wondered if that was some kind of taboo of the masters.

His interaction with other slaves came during meal times, taken in a larger room. It reminded Diego of the gatherings at fiestas or Saint's Day celebrations, where large quantities of food were prepared for many people and served on makeshift trestle tables outside. The biggest difference, the boy noted, was the lack of celebration, or even much conversation. Everyone seemed to size everyone else up when they weren't eating, as though no one trusted the other. Diego could see why. Some of the others were so alien as to not have any comparison with any of the animals he was familiar with in California.

There were several other Hoorinoo, almost identical to Phris. They hooted to one another as they entered the eating room but otherwise ignored each other. The other Hoorinoo were accompanied by other creatures, and Diego realized they were like Phris was to him; tutors of sorts. There were a few of the stick creatures and a creature that resembled a snake with legs. Two wolf-like creatures with a set of arms above their four legs were part of the group as well. There were two meal times, and at the second one, some of the slave students were so tired they could barely stay awake to finish their food.

A few days later, Diego pulled off the headphones, confident he could now ask the question that had been on his mind for a long time. "Why am I here? In this ship...a prisoner? Am I being ransomed?" That was a common custom among pirates and outlaws.

Phris made his shoulder shrug that indicated no. "You are not a prisoner, and you are not being held for ransom. What kind of ransom could your people pay that would satisfy the commander of a warship like this? You are a Seressin captive."

"Why, Phris? What am I to the Seressin?"

"Seressin take captives from all over the galaxy."

"But why?"

"They like others to…." Phris paused and glanced at one corner of the room. "They want to gather as many different kinds of people as they can. They believe that other races make good fighters, good workers." Phris's eyes begged for understanding. He was clearly uncomfortable with this subject.

Good slaves, thought Diego. "Were you captured?"

"I was sold," Phris replied, confirming Diego's suspicions.

"So we are slaves," the boy growled.

"Yes, Diego."

Phris's pronunciation of his name still made four distinct syllables instead of the three flowing ones that he had been used to all his life. He didn't mind. At least his friend called him by name, unlike others on board this ship. The name he heard most was "mrees."

"We are property of the Seressin, with the ability to work our way up in station. But yes, you are essentially correct," Phris added.

"'Mrees.' What does that mean, Phris?"

"Vermin. It is another name for slave."

"Am I the only one taken from my world?"

"I do not know, Diego. I have no knowledge of who is in the other pods," Phris answered.

"Pods?"

"Yes. Each ship like this has several pods or areas where the captured are held and taught, then assigned. You are the only one like you in this pod."

"What will they do to me?" Diego asked.

"I do not know, Diego. Maybe you will serve a Seressin.

Maybe a warrior. Perhaps they will make you wash clothes. I don't know."

Diego felt the horror turn to despair. He would be a servant washing clothes all his life? The thought threw a black cloud over his mind. He looked down at his hands, hands that were holding a device that was teaching him to be a good slave. Then he remembered Phris giving several possibilities.

"Learn, train hard, Diego," Phris interrupted his thoughts. "The masters decide what you will be after all you have learned and how you react to your training."

"How do I react?"

"Do the best you can and be yourself," Phris answered.

Diego sighed, then felt determination replace the despair. He put the headphones back on. He was a *hacendado's* son. He could ride as well as any vaquero, he had killed a wolf with a lariat and a knife, and he had branded, butchered, and herded his father's cattle. He would not remain a slave to a group of overgrown lizards.

During the next seven days, Diego attended small classes where four of them were taught basic fighting skills. The master in charge of each session showed the four slaves what moves he wanted, and then let the slaves practice among themselves while he watched. Most of the time this was a Seressin, but sometimes there was a master, or rejas, of another race. As the boy had been taught fist fighting by the vaqueros, the Seressin version wasn't hard to master. His problem most of the time was that some of the others were limber in places that made it hard for Diego to figure out the best moves. Still, he held his own and even won a few bouts.

A short time later, Diego was surprised, although Phris

claimed not to be, when the boy was assigned to the military training hall.

Chapter Three

"Mrees, take up the weapon!" the Grrlock ordered, pointing to a weapon's rack on one side of the room. The weapons in question were benign enough looking until one took in the long, flat blades at the end of each pole.

The Grrlock, a tall, broad-shouldered and muscular being, gazed at him with his emerald-green eyes. The eyes reminded Diego of cats' eyes. Indeed, the whole creature had more than a passing resemblance to the felines he was familiar with back in California. The gray fur was short, the slender fingers ended in claws, and his long tail lashed back and forth, waiting to see what he would do.

Diego perused the weapon. Standing on end, the staves were taller than he was with the sword-like blades shining dully. Miguel and his father had taught him to use a saber. Staves he had learned to use as well, but combined, he was not so sure. Diego had only seen this weapon, called an anfrees, on a teaching disk that showed him the preliminaries of use. He stepped to the rack and took the shortest one there, one that was still two inches taller than he was.

Moving his hands up and down the pole, he hefted it, getting the best balance. Then he turned to the Grrlock. "Do you wish to work with me, sir, or did you have something else in mind?" Diego asked with a confidence he didn't feel.

The Grrlock said nothing for a moment, staring at him with his crystal-green eyes. Then he growled, "Very well, puny one. We will spar against each other." Picking out a longer staff, the cat-like creature twirled it in his hands before going into the fighting stance crouch.

Diego also crouched, holding the staff loosely in front of him, watching the Grrlock. When the cat-man jumped forward, swinging the staff toward his head, the boy jerked his anfrees up to block. The staves clacked together, and Diego felt the shock of it through his arms and into his shoulders. He stepped back and then danced forward, swinging his weapon low, toward the Grrlock's legs, blade forward, but not quite enough to connect with the instructor's body. He needn't have worried.

With a growl, his opponent swung his staff down in a move almost too fast for Diego to see. This time the shock numbed his fingers, and the anfrees fell to the ground with a clatter. Almost instantly, the Grrlock's weapon sliced toward his head. Diego threw himself backward, and rolling on the floor, grabbed his fallen staff. Before he could get back up, though, he felt the tip of the other blade at the base of his throat.

"Cub, you need to learn more before you can compete with your master," the cat-man said. He pulled the weapon away from Diego's throat, and the boy rose.

Gazing unwaveringly at the Grrlock, Diego replied, "But, sir, is that not what I am here for; to learn from a rejas?"

The instructor blinked. For several heartbeats the cat-man stood quietly. Then he burst out in a howling laugh. "Not only are you a brave one, mrees, you also have a smooth and glib tongue. Take up your weapon, cub, and learn from a master."

For the next hour the two sparred, the Grrlock showing Diego various moves of offense, and more particularly, defense. At the end of the hour, Diego was sore and stiff, and feeling bruised from head to toe. However, he was satisfied with his new knowledge and the fact that he had held his own against the larger and more experienced warrior. At a motion from the instructor, Diego wiped down his anfrees, rubbing it as he had been instructed. He waited at semi-attention while the Grrlock did the same.

"What weapons are you familiar with?"

"I have practiced with a staff," Diego replied, using his own word for the Earth weapon. He showed him on an anfrees the difference. "I have also been taught to use a sword and a musket." Not knowing what the Seressin equivalents for those weapons were, Diego went through the motions of using each.

The Grrlock nodded and strode to a cabinet across the room. Diego followed the cat-man and gasped when he looked inside the cabinet. About a dozen swords hung gleaming in front of them. Most of them looked far more deadly than anything his father owned. Reaching in, Diego touched a narrow-bladed saber with a plain silver hilt.

"Take it up, cub, and show me what you have learned," the Grrlock told him.

Diego pulled out the sword and swished it in the air, moving his hand on the slightly oversized grip until it felt comfortable. Taking a few steps back and forth, he then turned and faced the Grrlock. He bowed, took his stance, and said softly, "I am ready, Rejas."

The Grrlock stepped forward and lunged with a saber longer and heavier than his. Diego parried the thrust easily and went on the offensive. The Grrlock effortlessly defended himself, and then made several offensive moves that were unfamiliar and more difficult for Diego to protect against. He was able to parry the instructor's thrusts. Though he never went on the offense again, Diego was able to hold his own.

Finally the Grrlock lowered his sword and stepped back. "Enough. You have done well, cub. You have a natural skill with the blade, as well as some experience. We will work more tomorrow." His instructor put away his weapon and turned back to Diego. "What is your name, cub?"

"Diego Perez y Andres Morales," the young man answered.

The cat-man blinked. "Such a large name for such a small youth."

"Diego is the name most used, Rejas," he explained meekly. "The names of the mother and the father are part of a person's full name. It is a custom among my people."

"Diego, then. I am Hreeshan."

"My thanks for the lesson, Rejas Hreeshan," Diego said formally, punctuating it with another bow.

"It is good to work with one so talented," Hreeshan replied. "I was not so sure at first."

"Sir?"

"I was skeptical of teaching one who had spent his first days cowering in a corner, crying."

Diego blushed and lowered his head. "It was so strange, Rejas. So different from my…home."

"Your destiny is not on a primitive planet, Diego, or you wouldn't have been selected."

Taking a chance, the boy looked up. "Will I ever see my father and mother again?"

"No."

Diego looked down again. He blinked away the threatening tears. Now was not the time to show emotion.

"You really are a cub, aren't you?" Hreeshan asked, more softly.

Diego nodded. "I am not fully grown, if that's what you mean, Rejas."

The instructor nodded. "How old are you in relation to manhood?"

"I am fourteen-years-old." Diego paused. "No. I was almost fifteen when I was captured. I would guess I am fifteen now." He had missed his birthday, he thought sadly. "Most of my people are considered men at seventeen to eighteen."

"Yes, just out of childhood," the Grrlock murmured, almost to himself. "Your destiny is here." He gazed directly into Diego's eyes. "Among the stars."

"Yes, sir," Diego responded dully.

"You can be great, cub. I see it in you," Hreeshan told him.

"How, Rejas? I am a mrees."

"Even a slave can achieve greatness," the Grrlock said, tugging his side whiskers. "I feel it in you."

Diego said nothing. What could he say? He was here, among these people who were so different from him. In a place so much stranger than his home.

"Cub…Diego. Work hard," Hreeshan said.

Diego looked into the Grrlock's eyes and saw sympathy. He bowed again before leaving.

Chapter Four

"The commander wants to watch the training, Diego," Phris told him early one day cycle. "Sometime in the next ship-week."

Diego could only guess, but as close as he could figure, he had been on the spaceship for three or four months. It was still hard to imagine that this place was moving among the stars, like a ship sailing across the ocean. Sometimes he wondered if he was outside, would he see God and His angels. He had tried to talk to Phris about it, but the lavender man shook his head, saying that he didn't believe that an all-powerful being resided in the same sphere that spaceships traveled through. Diego brought his mind back to Phris's announcement. "Commander?"

"Yes, the commander of the ship. He always checks out promising new trainees."

"And what if he likes me?"

"Then you would likely be serving in a position of power," Phris said. "Eventually."

Diego raised his eyebrows and asked, "But I will still be a slave, right?"

"Even slaves have been known to become masters," Phris philosophized. "I believe you will be one of those."

"All right, Phris, I will do my best." Diego didn't figure it was likely he could be a master among these people, but he would do his best, hoping he might become a well advanced slave at least.

"That is all you can do, my friend." His blue eyes showed pride in his protégé.

"And I will not forget what you have done when I become great and powerful," Diego said, his tone facetious.

"I thank you, Diego," Phris replied with a serious tone.

The next day cycle, Diego awoke early, showering and dressing before realizing breakfast was still more than an hour away. Phris had already left, as he had often since they had been assigned to the military hall. With a sigh, the young man looked in the small mirror that hung in the bathroom cubicle and wondered what to do with his time. He was too restless to lie back down. There was no library on this ship like the one he had at home, unless he counted the computer teaching room where he had been taught the space traveler's language. For some reason, Diego still didn't feel confident enough to walk the corridors and try to find something to learn on the computer.

He sat down on the edge of his bed. He wondered if he would be allowed to practice in the exercise room. It was closer. A short practice and then another quick shower would certainly make the time go faster.

Laying his palm on a special pad next to the door, he

walked into the empty corridor. He thought fleetingly of all the wondrous things he had seen and learned since his capture, but put them out of his mind. He had to focus on his lessons this morning so he would make a good impression on the commander. Diego walked the whole way to the practice center without seeing anyone. The vast room was also empty, and his steps echoed dully on the thinly padded floor. Approaching the weapon rack, he placed his hand on an identity pad, but this time nothing happened. Puzzled, Diego tried again, but with no success. Irritated, he stepped back. The racks must be kept locked during the rest cycle.

He was here. It was stupid to return to his room to simply sit and look at the bare cold walls. Pulling off his shoes, Diego walked to the cushioned exercise mat. After a few limbering exercises and several deep breaths, he began his workout. He kicked imaginary opponents, first with one leg, then leaping and kicking with both legs. This was followed by a tumbling routine that Diego was told was effective against armed, as well as unarmed, foes. He wasn't sure about that claim, but the discipline to make these moves had helped him in all of his other combat lessons. His concentration had improved, giving him the ability to focus on his body and what he wanted it to do.

Diego worked out for almost an hour and then stood quietly, listening to his heart beat and breathing. He was pleased that his lungs were pumping air evenly, and his heart was steady and not racing. Perhaps he had time for another exercise before going back to his cabin and cleaning up.

"What do you mean, coming here at this time, mrees?" a Seressin demanded.

Startled, Diego missed a step to begin a hand spring and landed heavily on the floor. His breath felt as though it had been sucked from his body. Standing over him, the Seressin loomed huge, the claws like knives outstretched and ready to rend him. The orange-red eyes bored into his own.

"Well?" he barked. "Why are you here? I see that you tried to get into the weapons cabinet. A mutiny? An assassination plot?" A dark green, scaled arm shot out and grabbed him, jerking Diego toward the Seressin warrior with astonishing speed. This time Diego didn't try to turn away. Instead, he gazed into the cat-like eyes, even though his heart hammered painfully in his chest.

"Why are you here?" the lizard-man growled again, shaking Diego hard enough to make his teeth rattle. Still dangling him up in the air, still shaking him, the Seressin walked several paces toward the door.

Diego tried futilely to get his tongue to work. Suddenly he was slammed against the wall, his head whipping back and banging painfully against the metal. His eyes blurred, and the room darkened for an instant. Desperate, Diego blinked and shook his head. Finally his voice returned. "I woke up early, Rejas. I thought I would practice what I had been taught."

The Seressin continued to hold him against the wall, studying him. The only sound in the room was their breathing. Then slowly, the boy was lowered to the ground. "Perhaps."

Diego stood quietly.

"Hmm," the reptile warrior said after what felt like an eternity. "Maybe it is as you said. Go now. You have other duties to attend to."

Diego left, resisting the urge to run. He walked as fast as

decorum would allow.

"It is duly noted that you wish to study and practice on your own time. This room and the learning chamber will be open to you," the Seressin said.

Diego turned, almost gaping, but he remembered his teaching and bowed, knees bent and head lowered. He had been told this was an adaptation of submission posture for those being executed. Somehow Diego thought some underlings were still executed this way.

"Do not do anything to betray our trust," the Seressin added.

"Yes, sir."

Diego reached for the door pad. It seemed like forever before the door slid open. As soon as it did, Diego slipped out and returned to his room. For once, the tiny cubicle felt welcoming and safe. Diego sat down, shaken by his near disaster. *Why did the master give me permission?* He could understand being manhandled; that was the Seressin way. The demon creatures had done it before. But concessions to a slave? Diego shook his head, determined to make the best of the situation.

Finally he stood up and, looking in the tiny mirror, combed his hair. He pulled off his sweaty clothes and tossed them on the bunk. Then he splashed water on his face and neck, dried off, and put on a clean outfit. Smiling at his reflection, Diego turned and left the little room.

***

For several days, Diego wondered when the commander would come and watch him practice with the sword, the corlin (a pistol that shot a deadly kind of light), the anfrees, or simply with his hands and feet in unarmed combat. He asked Phris, but his friend shrugged and said, "When the master chooses."

Testing his newfound liberty, Diego made periodic excursions to the learning center either before or after the sleep cycle. Phris had taught him enough so that he could run the machines himself. At first the young man picked spools at random, ogling at information about alien races beyond his imagination. Other beings came to the center, but for the most part, they ignored Diego. As he learned, though, he was able to recognize some of the creatures identified on his learning spools. He also saw stars expand and explode before his eyes. Diego witnessed battles that made the skirmishes of his homeland seem like child's play. Even the duels were more deadly and intense.

Finally Diego found a spool that gave background about the reptile-like masters, the Seressin. It showed the Seressin home planet, a dry, warm place, not too unlike the California of his memories. He watched a blood-red sun rise over one horizon and later set over another. Emerald-colored lakes sporadically dotted a hilly landscape. Turquoise-hued bushes covered a great deal of the land.

Dragon-like creatures thundered over a distant hill, bugling to one another. One of the dragons, which appeared to be the size of horses, suddenly broke off from the rest of the herd and ran toward him. As it came closer, Diego had to remind himself that these were moving pictures and not real. The dragon was covered with shimmering blue-green scales and had small deep-blue horns between its up-pricked, pointed ears. It jerked to one side and then pivoted back, barely missing a stride. Its feet were cloven like a deer's.

It was then that Diego saw a furred, bushy-tailed creature, about the size of a bobcat, running back and forth, obviously trying to outrun the dragon. Another dragon came from the opposite direction and cut off the smaller creature's escape. Soon Diego was hearing the death cries of the furred creature. Muttered hooting was all he heard before the two dragon-like creatures began eating. Their orange eyes glared at him when they lifted their heads from their kill. Long, tapering tails twitched.

A rumbling noise in the distance caused the dragons to jerk their heads up. With angry hoots the creatures ran toward the distant red-gold hills. The rumbling grew louder, and a transportation device came into view. It was large and box-like on solid wheels, entirely enclosed. Diego had seen several similar type vehicles on other information spools, so this one didn't surprise him. What did surprise him were the Seressin who got out when the door opened in the vehicle. Three of the reptilians walked around, examining the ground. Then they looked up, seemingly right at him. After a moment, they pulled boxes from the vehicle and proceeded to sit down and eat.

Puzzled, Diego continued to watch, seeing slight differences between the individuals on the screen in front of him. One of the Seressin had slightly bluish cheek patches. Another one's claws were bright orange, matching its eyes. The third was smaller, but stockier than the rest.

In shock, Diego realized that the blue patched one was the same Seressin who had allowed him access to this room and the weapons practice room. The scene reminded him of the times when he and his brother and sisters had gone out by the lake with their mother to have a picnic. Was this the master's family? Diego watched a little longer and saw the orange-clawed one reach over and touch the master on the cheek. The stocky one occasionally said things Diego couldn't understand, and then it barked in laughter. The spool went on for a while longer before it ended with the group packing up and getting back into the vehicle. He stared at the blank screen for a few minutes, then he took the spool to the tray and put it away. Other spools had similar symbols, and he picked one.

Over the next few days, Diego learned about the Seressin land, the people, and their cities. He learned that honor was extremely important, even more than among his people. Diego was surprised to learn that not all Seressin were warriors, only those who commanded and manned the spaceships. The Seressin culture was complex, with teachers and businessmen held on as high a plane as the warriors and commanders. Even those had received military training.

As the days passed, Diego found himself in the learning center earlier and earlier, fascinated by the myriad of alien planets. Most spools containing music, art, and science either didn't interest him or were far beyond his ability to understand. Some spools contained information on numerous varieties of martial arts forms and strategies of combat, and Diego avidly studied those, practicing some of the techniques in the exercise room. During all this time, Diego still wondered when the high rejas was going to watch him.

Chapter Five

Commander Ziron gazed through the view port to the exercise room where various captives were working out. He watched the most recent captive carefully, his clawed finger scratching his blue cheek patch. His scientists told him this being was designated human, a mammalian of small importance.

"Who taught him breerol movements?" he asked his companion, Hreeshan, the Grrlock slave master.

"No one that I am aware of, Marix," came the reply. "Perhaps he learned it from another slave."

Ziron shook his head. "I have had his movements closely monitored. He had to have learned from a teaching spool."

Hreeshan's whiskers quivered. "He does spend a great deal of time in the learning center. It would appear that he has learned well."

"The Bremmer is promising, Commander Ziron," another Seressin, one slightly shorter and stockier, said.

"Yes, he is, but I tend toward the human," Ziron rumbled.

"The human?" the Seressin barked. "I think he is weak. All he does is study spools. He will run at the first sign of real danger. You saw him after his capture. He will endanger you, my lord. Pick another squire."

"Nevertheless, I think he is promising," Ziron replied, a note of finality in his voice.

"His training then?" Hreeshan asked.

"As is for now."

Ziron made a motion with his taloned finger. The others left the observation room. He continued to watch the alien adolescent. He remembered his hris drink induced dream; the one where this boy figured predominantly. For some reason he could not forget or ignore it. Ziron continued to watch the human until the session was over, then he left, determined that this slave should be his next squire.

***

Several day cycles later, Hreeshan taught the recruits on the anfrees. He sparred personally with Diego at the beginning of the session, then abruptly called a halt to the workout.

"But we have barely begun the session, Rejas," Diego blurted out. He wondered if he had done something to offend the weapon's master.

"This training period is over, cub," the Grrlock said, looking over the group. "Assignments have been made." He returned his gaze to the human. "You are assigned to be Commander Ziron's junior squire, Diego."

The other trainees appeared shocked, and some showed signs of jealousy.

"What? He never observed me!"

Hreeshan laughed, his yowling echoing off the walls.

"But he has, cub. He has watched you often. For many day cycles he has scrutinized you. It is almost as though he feels some kind of bond with you." The Grrlock bent down closer to Diego's face. "Do not disappoint him. Do not make him regret his decision."

"I will do my best, Rejas," Diego said solemnly. Then he paused, pondering. "Rejas, is Commander Ziron the Seressin with blue on his cheeks?"

"Yes, Diego. He commands this ship. It is a great honor for you to be chosen."

Diego noticed some of the animosity on the faces of the other recruits, but ignored them. "What do I do now?"

"Follow his instructions explicitly. Serve him as well as you can. You will be taught by masters in all the arts of being a squire."

Diego thought of all the stories of knights and squires from his world's history, and wondered if there was any similarity between the two.

"You will receive your new quarter's assignment and meet your new training masters tomorrow."

Hreeshan turned to the others and gave them their assignments. Most of his fellow trainees were assigned as junior squires to sub-commanders. Another was assigned to work with the ship's armament master, and the others to the small craft flight school.

The next morning as Diego sat in the teaching center trying to concentrate on another spool, he asked Phris, "What do I need to do to please the commander?"

"Work hard, as you have been doing. Be honest with the commander. Follow his commands explicitly. It is almost unheard of for a primitive world first year slave to be selected as a command staff squire. It is a great honor, Diego."

Diego looked at the floor, wondering why the commander picked him. "You sound like Master Hreeshan. Is there something I should know about being a squire? Something that will keep the commander from getting angry with me?" Diego asked, remembering the incident in the training room.

Phris hooted with amusement. "There is nothing that will keep a Seressin commander from becoming angry when he is so inclined." The little humanoid grew solemn when Diego didn't share the humor of his joke. "All you can do is your best, Diego."

He nodded. He had thought that would be the answer Phris would give him. Putting the headphones back on, Diego turned his attention back to the language spool and concentrated on the words it was teaching him.

As the spool ended, Diego felt a tap on his shoulder. He turned and saw a skeletal-looking Bressinin beckoning to him. "Come," it muttered.

Diego looked at Phris, but the furry alien motioned for him to go with the creature. "May I ask who is summoning me?" he asked the slender alien.

"The commander," came the answer.

The multi-jointed man lurched out of the room, and Diego followed, his heart beginning to race in nervous anticipation. Down familiar corridors they strode, then into an elevator. When it opened, they went down hallways totally unfamiliar to the boy. He guessed this was the masters' living or working quarters. The corridors were the same metallic grey, but they were wider.

The Bressinin stopped at a doorway and touched the identification plate. When the door slid open, Diego saw an oval-shaped table in the middle of a large room, chairs all around it. There were several Seressin sitting there, gazing at him. Hreeshan and two other Grrlocks, as well as a few other aliens, were also sitting at the table.

One of the Seressin motioned to him. Without hesitation, Diego walked up to the commander and bowed low before him. "I live only to obey you, Commander," Diego said formally. He raised his eyes just enough to see the commander's response.

Commander Ziron was dressed from the neck down in some kind of suit that resembled armor. It had a blue-gray metallic sheen and seemed to be made of finely woven links. On the clawed hands were gauntlets with the finger tips removed, showing the Seressin's red painted claws. Diego recognized the outfit as one of ceremonial dress during times of war. He knew it was also the proper garb for the ritual of induction. A warrior's non-plumed but crested helmet sat on the table in front of the commander, the cheek plates shining a golden-bronze color.

The Seressin nodded. "You have learned well, tre-ol. Now stand before me and listen well." Ziron motioned to the Seressin at his side.

"Tre-ol," the reptile intoned.

Diego noticed that this one's eyes were darker than the others.

"Give me your birth name."

"Diego Perez y Andres Morales," he declared proudly.

"A large name for such a small tre-ol. Hopefully, you

will grow into such a proud name," Commander Ziron said, gurgling with soft laughter.

Diego blushed.

The darker-eyed Seressin, whom Diego realized was a sub-commander, continued. "Diego Perez y Andres Morales, you have been chosen as Commander Ziron's squire. It is your duty to serve him even to the sacrifice of your life for him. You will obey explicitly, and you will bring honor to the commander's ship with your service. You will not shirk your duties. You will fight valiantly and with bravery. Do you understand and agree?"

"Yes. I will serve honorably and well—even to the giving of my life." He bowed again deeply, not even raising his head the slightest amount.

"Well answered, Diego, my squire," Ziron answered.

Straightening up, Diego stood quietly waiting.

Ziron turned to his sub-commander, the one who had administered the oath. His jaws opened wide in a grimacing smile, showing long dark teeth. "See, Morgol. I told you he would know the procedure."

"It takes more than words to make a good squire, and it takes more than spool learning, too," Morgol grumbled, his eyes still boring into Diego's.

"So it does, so it does," Ziron replied. "But the comet and the stars have all chosen this one. I can do no less then follow their course."

Morgol nodded, but his eyes were still filled with suspicion.

Ziron's growling laugh broke the sub-commander's scrutiny. "Morgol, if you are so adamant about the Treesh youth, take him as your squire. You two have well matched ambitions."

Morgol grunted. "Very well, Commander. I will, even though the Treesh is better suited to squire a ship's commander than a subordinate. And he'd certainly be a better squire for you than a scrawny, soft-skinned mammalian."

"Ah, but sub-commander, you intend to be a commander someday, do you not? That would make your choice meaningful."

This time Morgol said nothing, but Diego wondered if these two were as friendly as they sounded. For some reason, even though Ziron had been rough with him before, Diego trusted the ship's commander. He did not trust Morgol, and he wondered about the Treesh. He knew what creature Lord Ziron was referring to — a sinewy, sharp fanged, green-skinned alien. Somehow, Diego realized he would need to be on his guard around the Treesh. Like most of his race, the reptilian was moody and vicious, even more than the Seressin. The boy had seen it lash out in anger more than once, injuring those he laid claws on.

"Diego, you will be working with me," Hreeshan said. "Your quarters will be on this level. Gather what belongings you have and return to the squire meeting room by the mid-meal. After mid-meal you will report to the quartermaster for fitting of proper attire and armor. You will be expected to attend Ship Commander Ziron at the end meal. Ufers will guide you to your new quarters."

"Yes, Rejas," Diego said, bowing to Commander Ziron before following the Bressinin out of the room.

"Remember your way, young Quirlis. I will not stay with

you to lead you back," the skeletal being admonished. "And do not be late to the quartermaster."

As the elevator door opened, the Bressinin motioned him out with a croaking sort of grunt. Knowing his time was limited, Diego trotted to the small cubicle he had been sharing with Phris. The lavender man was waiting.

"Hurry, Diego! I have your clothes and things packed. There is little time before the mid-meal." Phris's hooting words were almost sibilant in their rush. "You must not be late for your first duties, my fine squire; Quirlis."

Diego looked at the fuzzy little alien in gratitude. "Thank you, Phris." He clasped his friend/teacher's shoulder. "Thank you for all you have done. I'll try to come and see you when I can."

"Serve well, and you will bring honor to me; to all of us down here," Phris hooted. "And I have enjoyed your companionship. Maybe we will meet again someday." He blinked, his blue eyes looking watery. "Now, you must hurry." Phris shoved the bundle into Diego's arms and pushed him out the door. He followed him down the corridor and to the elevator. Reaching up to the control panel, Phris pushed an orange-colored button. "May the bright smiling deities go with you, Diego," he said.

As the door slid shut, Diego called out, "*Vaya con Dios*, Phris."

The elevator felt lonely, and suddenly he wasn't as excited as he had been earlier. The door opened, and he stepped into the corridor. There were symbols on the wall, but to his chagrin, Diego realized that he had not learned the Seressin writing. Turning to his right, Diego made his way toward the conference room where he had sworn his loyalty oath to Commander Ziron, hoping to see someone to ask.

After what felt like an interminable amount of time, Diego finally found a Bressinin. "The squire's meeting room?"

"Signs on the corridor walls," it croaked, pointing.

"I...I can't read them," Diego admitted.

It made a creaking sound that the boy took to be laughter. Diego blushed.

"You cannot be serious. You are the commander's new squire, and you cannot read?"

"I was never taught."

The bony shoulders wriggled, and the Bressinin pointed. "Down this corridor, past the elevator, continue. Corridor to right—at the end. It is a large room."

Nodding his thanks, Diego dashed down the corridor, knowing that it was well into the mid-meal. He dodged various creatures who seemed to materialize just to delay him. *Why couldn't all these people have been around when I got off the elevator?* Finally he arrived at the large room and dashed in, panting.

Hreeshan grabbed him and shoved him against the wall. His bundle fell on the floor. "A fine entrance for your first assignment under the commander," he hissed.

"I...got lost, sir," Diego stammered.

"Lost? Lost? A quirlis offers no excuses. He only obeys and gets the job done."

Diego expected surliness from the taciturn Seressin, but such anger from the normally even-tempered Grrlock was a surprise to him. He grabbed his bundle.

"Never mind, we have to get your uniform."

Hreeshan jerked him toward the far end of the room and through a door, approaching a barrel-shaped creature that stood staring balefully at them. The one, large-pupiled green eye startled him. Its gaze was penetrating. Stiff, bristly hair stood up several inches above the alien's head, and huge pointed ears quivered as they approached. When it opened its mouth, round peg-like teeth greeted him, bright orange and uneven. His arms reached the floor. The legs were half the length of the arms, and Diego wondered how the man would be able to run if a fire broke out.

"Quickly, the squire needs to be fitted for uniforms. And we need something for him to wear to attend the commander at the end meal."

"It would be easier if the squire had been here earlier," the quartermaster grumbled.

The next few minutes were frantic, with the quartermaster holding various measuring instruments up to his body; up, down, and around. Finally he finished and sent Diego behind a screen. After some rummaging sounds and grumbling, the alien came back, several sets of clothing in his long-fingered hands.

"Here," he muttered, shoving the pile into the young man's arms.

Diego almost dropped his bundle of personal belongings at his surprise. This creature was fast!

"I will have your permanent attire ready in a few ship cycles...if you are still squire then," he added, his laughter rumbling softly from his squat frame.

If? Diego thought. "Thank you," was what he actually said.

"Hurry!" Hreeshan ordered on the other side of the screen. "It is beyond time to meet with the protocol master, and then if there is time, you will meet the other squires."

But there was not time. Diego had a minute to jerk off his old uniform and throw on the metallic black tunic trimmed with silver piping, along with the tight dark-violet pants and silver ankle length boots. Then he was rushed into a large room that resembled the teaching room on the other level.

There were already several other beings, including one who looked like the commander. This one, however, had a long sinuous tail and yellow scales, something the Seressin did not have, and knobby horns on top of its head. There were several of the cat-like Grrlocks, and another creature he had never seen before, a slug-like being. Nearest him was a Breanth, an alien completely covered in course dark fur, with wolfish ears and snout. The Breanth opened its jaws in a smile that Diego couldn't tell if it was threatening or friendly. The teeth were just as sharp and numerous as those of wolves or coyotes on Earth. The Seressin-like creature, which Diego recognized as the Treesh previously spoken of, gazed malevolently at him. It hissed, a long drawn out sound like that of a nest of angry snakes. Then it, too, grinned, showing two long fangs and a row of smaller, needle sharp teeth.

"You are late, Quirlis Diego," a tinny voice spoke to him from a table on the far side of the room. Diego looked in the direction of the voice and found himself staring at a box similar to the teaching machines on the slaves' level. "Well, boy, take your place!" it ordered.

Standing next to the table stood a slack-eyed, grey-skinned being with a hunched back. It didn't move. Diego wondered if he should stand next to him or find a seat.

"Take your place!"

"That means sit down, mrees," the Treesh hissed.

Diego shot an irritated look at the reptilian and looked back toward the machine. "Where is my place, Rejas," he asked hesitantly.

"In a Grisolian garbage heap," the Treesh said under his breath. The slug-like creature on the other side rumbled a laugh.

"Next to Quirlis Wors," the machine answered.

"Me," muttered the Breanth, motioning with one clawed finger to an empty seat.

Gratefully, Diego nodded and sat down.

"I am Rejas Anaar. I will be teaching protocol and etiquette." The box paused. "In other words, if you listen and remember, I will be prolonging your lives as squires for the ship's officers." There was a tinny chuckle. "As you are all newly selected, we will begin with the basics. By the way, I will not repeat myself. We are too far behind as it is."

Several heads turned toward Diego before the machine spoke again. In the next few hours, Diego learned more than he ever thought possible about the serving of the evening meal to the commander and his sub-commanders. He learned that he must stand so many paces behind and to the side of the commander while Ziron was eating. There was a certain way one picked up the dirty dishes, and certain beverages to eat with different types of food.

The commander's cloris, or badge of rank, was cared for by the squire at certain points during the meal. Utensils were changed often, hand towels presented just so. By the time the meal was actually ready to be served, Diego's head was swimming. Of course, it didn't help that he hadn't eaten since first meal.

Nervously Diego led the small group of junior squires into the commander's mess, where the tables had already been set with goblets, plates, and bowls. He assisted the kitchen help with placing the eating utensils, and then went through the procedures to check for anything that might have been left to harm the commander. Diego really had no idea what he was looking for, but he did see a strange looking box, about the size of his fingernail, on one of the chair legs. Carefully he peeled it away and handed it to the guard at the doorway.

The alien, a squatty, round-faced, barrel-chested man with skin like tree bark, threw back his head and bellowed his laughter. "You found what could have been a device, young Quirlis, but you would have blown us all up if it had been real."

"This tiny thing?" Diego asked. The guard glowered. Diego ducked his eyes briefly in chagrin, then looked back up at the alien. "Then what should I have done?" He heard the hissing laughter of the Treesh behind him.

"Anaar didn't tell you procedure, did he?"

"He said a great many things, but I guess I didn't remember them all," Diego answered softly. He vaguely remembered the box talking about things that would harm the commanders, and assumed that he was supposed to get rid of them.

The guard grunted. "Next time you tell me. I have been trained to recognize and deal with anything that might be used against a starship commander."

Diego peered closely at the tiny metallic device. "What could something this little do?"

The guard gazed at him in amazement. "You have no idea. What do they do on your world to assassinate leaders? Ask them to shoot themselves?" He rumbled in pleasant laughter.

Diego couldn't help himself. He found himself smiling. "I have heard of poison; some have been shot or stabbed."

"A first generation mrees from a primitive world." The alien sighed. "Well, a device this size and shape could hold enough poison gas to kill everyone in the room. Or if it was a bomb, it could blow a hole in the ship that would suck us out into space."

"Oh," was all Diego could say. He continued to stare at the thing that was smaller than a Mexican centavo. He had learned so much in so little time, but Diego was realizing that there was much, much more knowledge he needed to survive in this strange place.

"That is what comes of letting a first generation mrees become a squire," hissed the Treesh from behind him.

The guard growled a warning to the creature and then addressed Diego. "Perhaps when we both have free time, I can teach you more about the kind of devices you need to watch out for. After all, it is something you need to know in order to protect the commander."

Diego smiled his gratitude. Quickly, he checked the rest of the commander's place to make sure all was in order. A soft chime sounded, and the young man took his place two steps behind the left side of the chair.

Chapter Six

The commander and ten subordinates filed in. Diego pulled his master's chair out and waited for Ziron to stand in front of it. Then Diego pushed it in as the commander sat down. It was much like what he had done for his mother back home. He forced that memory out of his mind.

The rest of the meal went smoothly, and Diego remembered everything he was supposed to do. The new squire was feeling as though he might survive this first evening of service when Ziron made a request.

"Get my after dinner drink."

"Which one is that, Rejas?"

"Prasian flame juice," Ziron answered. "It is labeled." He pointed toward the kitchen.

"Yes, sir," Diego said, inclining his head and dashing off. Inside the kitchen, Diego rushed toward one of the cooks. "Prasian flame juice," he panted. "Where is it?"

"Over there," the cook grunted, pointing a long, yellow-tipped finger toward a rack on the far wall. In dismay, Diego examined the bottles and canisters that filled the rack. He studied and pondered. The symbols on the containers were totally incomprehensible to him. Flame juice. He looked for something that might look like an orange or red-colored liquid, but some of the bottles were opaque. He grabbed a bottle with a thick, viscous-looking liquid and headed toward the door. *But what if I'm wrong?*

"Excuse me, but is this it?" he asked the cook.

"No, you young idiot! Do you want to burn the commander's gullet? That is blood vinegar!" The cook pointed to a small rack set slightly apart. All the bottles were the same.

"This?" he asked. The cook nodded and, cradling the bottle, Diego dashed back to the dining hall. Carefully trying to avoid acting nervous, the boy poured the dark orange liquid into a tall glass.

Suddenly, the commander's clawed hand shot out and grabbed his wrist. Diego almost dropped the bottle, but he managed to hang onto it and even avoided spilling any of the liquid. The commander's grip tightened, and Diego winced in pain. He bit his lip as a claw dug into his skin, and a small drop of blood welled up and then dropped into the glass of liquid.

Diego felt his heart stopping in fear and his breath catching from the pain. Finally Ziron released his iron grip. "You were too slow," he muttered, his red-gold eyes glinting with anger.

"My apologies, Lord Commander," Diego replied, his voice soft to hide the tremble of humiliation. He reached for the cup. "I will get you a new cup, sir."

Ziron grasped it, bringing it to his jaws, where he drank the liquor in two gulps. "Now pour more."

"Yes, Rejas," he said, resisting the temptation to shudder. Would the commander eat him if he served poorly? Was that more than a message of dissatisfaction? Diego poured the drink to a certain point and stopped when Ziron made a gesture.

"Put the bottle back and then go to my quarters," he instructed. To the others he said, "Send all the squires out."

Diego bowed and left. When he went out to the corridor, he saw the Treesh, the Breanth, the Grrlock, and several other squires. Most of them were new squires, like himself, whom he had been studying with, but there were some he didn't recognize. Diego wondered if they were older squires.

The Treesh leaned against the wall, his arms folded across his chest, a sneer on his leathery lips. "A worthy beginning, mrees," he hissed.

Anger flared, but Diego squelched it. An argument now, just outside the dining hall, would not endear him to his commander. Besides, he had been given an order. "I thought I did rather well considering that I am a first year mrees from a primitive planet," he said, gazing directly into the yellow eyes. "Excuse me, but the commander made a request, and I am honor bound to obey him."

The Treesh did not move, and for a moment, neither did anyone else. Then the Breanth moved aside, and the young Grrlock motioned to him. "Ah, Quirlis, I wish to ask you a question. May I accompany you?" he asked.

Diego nodded. As they walked down the corridor and around the corner, the human turned to his cat-like companion and said, "Thank you…?"

"Rreengrol is my name. And you?"

"Diego Perez y Andres Morales."

"Are you called by that whole name? Even by friends?" Rreengrol asked, a slight purr deep in his throat.

"No. Diego is my common name. Can I consider you my friend?"

"Yes, unless you do something to break that friendship," Rreengrol answered.

Smiling, Diego continued to walk down the corridor. "Good point." Then he stopped in shock. "I don't know where the commander's quarters are." Panic started to slide into his gut.

"Then we ask, or better yet, we read the idents on the walls."

Diego sighed, but said nothing.

"Or is part of the problem that you cannot read?" Rreengrol asked in a low voice.

"I can read. I can read my own language, but I cannot read the commander's," Diego finally admitted. "And after my mistake at the last meal, I can't afford to make any more mistakes."

"If it will help, let me tell you that if the commander had been truly upset, you would probably have awakened in the infirmary," Rreengrol growled, his upper lip curled back in what Diego guessed was a grin.

"Yes, that does help. Thanks."

"Here is the commander's quarters, Diego," the Grrlock said, pointing toward a door.

Diego studied the door emblem carefully, noting each of the strokes and the order they were placed on the door. He put his hand on the identity plate. The door slid aside for him.

"I will leave you now, my new friend. And I would suggest that you ask Anaar to teach you to read. I think he would be happy to."

"Thanks again, Rreengrol," Diego said as he stepped inside.

The door hissed shut behind him. He looked around the room. It was fairly austere, with nothing that Diego would consider artistic decoration. Neither was there anything he would consider religious. The only things on the wall were weapons. One small alcove held a computer, a rack of spools next to it. There were a few chairs, lightly upholstered with bright yellow cloth, and one couch against the far wall. There were small tables on either end of the couch and beside the chairs. Several packets of papers lay on the largest table. Diego glanced at them, but didn't touch them. There were no pictures anyway, but even if there had been, he would have hesitated. There were the commander's, and he didn't want to eavesdrop.

There was another area off the main room, and Diego walked into it. A contoured bed sat on one side of the room, another table, and a wardrobe set into a wall. The door swished open when he approached. Uniforms hung there, most utilitarian, some ornate with jewels and metallic braid. Turning, Diego saw a monitor set into the wall opposite the bed. It was dark at the moment. He wondered what he was supposed to do until the commander returned.

Remembering what the servants in his own house in California did, Diego checked the bed. It was already made. He went back to the wardrobe and, as the door slid open, Diego took out an outfit. Checking for lint or dirt, the boy smiled crookedly at the thought of doing something he would have disdained a few months ago. The suit was clean. He put it back and pulled out another uniform. It, too, looked clean, but Diego checked anyway. He was straightening a small line of braid when he felt a heavy clawed hand on his shoulder. The pressure of the grip almost made him gasp.

"What are you doing with my uniform?" Ziron demanded, his voice an angry hiss.

The grip tightened, and Diego did gasp. His fingers began to tingle with numbness, but he kept a tight grip on the uniform, determined not to let it fall to the ground. "Where I come from, the servants care for their master's things, Rejas," Diego said quickly, biting his lips against the pain of Commander Ziron's claws. The grip loosened so quickly that Diego staggered back, but he still held on to the uniform.

Ziron gazed at him, a slightly puzzled look in his eyes. "You are not a servant. You are my squire. I have slaves to care for my clothing."

"But I was told I am a slave, Rejas."

"Even slaves have rank," the reptilian snapped. "When you care for anything other than my life, you will care for my weapons." The Seressin followed the boy's gaze to the weapons on the wall. "But that will happen when you have learned more about them."

Diego hung the uniform back in the wardrobe without taking his eyes from his master's gaze. "My apologies, Rejas," Diego replied.

"Never apologize needlessly, Quirlis," Ziron admonished.

Diego nodded. "Yes, sir."

"Anytime I require you to come to my cabin without me,

you will check to make sure all is secure. Otherwise, you rest and wait," the commander instructed.

"Yes, sir."

"There will be times you will be required to remain with me all night. There will be times when I will instruct you in your duties myself." The Seressin stopped and stared hard at Diego. "You will be available at anytime when I call. In order to do that, you will need this."

Ziron handed Diego what appeared to be a plain brooch. Its shape was that of a tiny rainbow, but it sparkled more like a field of stars. Seeing something similar attached to the commander's chest below the left shoulder, Diego gazed at the back of the pin and then attached it to his own shirt in a similar position.

"When I summon you like this...." Ziron touched the jewel at the top of his pin, and a tiny chime sounded from Diego's pin.

The boy also felt a small shock through the shirt where the pin was attached, and reached up to tap his pin.

"Excellent, Diego. That is exactly what you do." The commander's voice echoed small and tinny from Diego's pin. "I will tell you my location, and you will report to me at once."

Again, Diego nodded. "Yes, Rejas."

"Quirlis, you will address me as Marix. That is my title as a starship commander."

"Yes, Marix." Diego bowed. Then he looked into Ziron's amber-orange eyes. "Marix, is it permitted to do extra studying during sleep time? There is so much I still need to learn."

"Sleep time? No, if you are to be my squire, you must be rested."

"Yes, Marix." Diego despaired not being able to learn the written language.

"What is it you need to learn, Quirlis, that you would give up sleep and perhaps jeopardize my life? You do realize that a squire is life-bound to his master, do you not? You have pledged your life to mine. Did you not listen to the oath you made?" Ziron's eyes glinted with irritation, and he leaned forward, his face within inches of Diego's.

Chapter Seven

A sudden surge of fear, a remembrance of his first encounters with the Seressin, almost froze his tongue. "No. No, Marix," Diego stammered. "I have not forgotten. But...." He paused. "When you asked for the drink, I almost got something dangerous for you. I...I couldn't read the labels, Marix." Diego felt his cheeks redden in his embarrassment.

Ziron drew back, and his breath hissed between sharp teeth. His eyes hardened, and Diego wondered if he had just demoted himself.

"I was told you had all the basic knowledge. It was too good to be true, you having everything you needed in a quarter of a ship's year." Ziron turned away and walked toward the main room.

"Do you want your pin back, Marix?" Diego asked meekly.

"What!?" Ziron roared, turning and shoving his face into the boy's again. "Are you quitting?"

Fright exploded in his chest, but Diego didn't flinch.

"But...but I cannot serve you if I am a danger to you."

Ziron didn't blink. His eyes bored into Diego's. "Do you want to be my squire?" he demanded.

"Yes, Marix. I do!"

"Then you will find a way to supplement your education—during your free time, not your sleep time." Ziron paced. Then he stopped and faced the boy again. "If you are unwilling to do that, then you might as well hand me that communicator badge and crawl back down to the slaves' quarters. Then everyone on this ship will know that all you are good for is to clean uniforms and make beds."

The words stung, and despite his fear, Diego drew himself up. "Marix, a member of the Morales family does not shirk or shrink from honorable duty," he declared, his voice determined, but cracking.

"So honor is of importance to your race, too." Ziron pulled back, apparently satisfied.

"Yes, Marix, to most humans, anyway."

Ziron stood silent, his eyes still studying his squire. Then he threw his head back and barked out loud laughter. "I think you are right, Quirlis Diego." He laughed for several minutes, then he was as serious as before. "Do not disappoint me or the comet," he said tersely.

Comet? Diego wondered at the reference. "I will do my best, Marix Ziron."

"Good. I have too much to do to be selecting a new squire every quarter year." His eyes now glinted gold with satisfaction.

Diego took a chance. "Marix, are there other squires I will need to work with? Someone with more, uh, experience?"

The boy had wondered why Ziron didn't have more than one squire, or why he would choose someone as green as Diego.

Ziron sighed, a sibilant sound. "My last squire failed me. He cared more about his own survival and well-being than his commander's. I had my reasons for choosing you, Quirlis."

Diego wasn't about to ask anything else.

"Use some of your weaponry time for the next ten ship days, then you can double your efforts with weapons."

"Thank you, Marix."

"Make sure you do not fall behind. Now go to your cabin. I believe your route takes you by the study hall."

"Yes, Marix," Diego said. He bowed and turned toward the outer door. As he walked through the doorway and felt the soft stirring of air from its closing, Diego pondered the commander's words. "Anaar," he whispered.

Rreengrol had mentioned Anaar as well. Diego would ask the teacher box. Perhaps he would be willing to help. Diego remembered the route he had taken with the Grrlock to get to the commander's quarters. He retraced his steps to the dining hall and then to the education center. As soon as the door opened, the lights automatically came on, and Anaar's eyes lit up.

"What is it you need, Quirlis Diego?"

"I am sorry to bother you, Rejas," Diego began.

"I never sleep, Diego, therefore I am available at any time," Anaar stated.

"Never sleep?"

"I am a machine. My circuits rest at times, but sleep as you know it is foreign to me," Anaar replied.

"A machine?" Diego was flabbergasted. "But who puts in

the spools to make you run? How do you know what to say?"

"The machines that use spools are computers. I am an android. I have a brain. It was manufactured, but it is a brain nevertheless," Anaar explained patiently.

"Oh."

"What is it you wish?" the android repeated.

"I need to learn to read the Seressin language," Diego said. "But I have to do it during my free time, whenever that is."

For half a moment, the android studied him, the blue eyes steady and calculating. "Yes, there are gaps in your education that could be a detriment to your master."

Diego wasn't sure all the words that the teacher had used, but he knew Anaar was agreeing with him.

"There is one point two cycles before you begin your sleep session. We can start now," Anaar said.

It wasn't much, but Diego nodded, grateful for the teacher's help. By the time he had to leave for his cabin, though, the young squire was pleased. He had learned many base glyphs, and had begun to put some of them together into phrases that he typed into the computer.

Anaar agreed. "A very good beginning, Diego." The android turned to one of the computers and spoke a command in a language the boy could not understand. A piece of paper came out of one side. "Take it and study. If you learn these, they will form the basis for the next hundred glyphs and their compounds."

Hundred? Diego thought. Spanish hadn't been that hard to learn to read. "A hundred more?" he asked aloud.

"Oh, yes, you have learned the most basic glyphs this

evening. You are a quick learner, Diego," Anaar told him.

"Thank you, sir," Diego said, proud but anxious about the job ahead of him. This was all so daunting. He looked at the paper in his hand, the tiny lines representing the pictures next to them.

"Come to me during your next evening free time, and I will teach you more glyphs. When you have all the base glyphs in your mind, we can use sleep memory disks to teach you more quickly."

"Sleep memory disks?" Diego asked, puzzled.

"You will see," Anaar said enigmatically. "You must go to your cabin before you are put on report. The commander is adamant about his subordinates following schedules and rules."

Diego wanted to ask Anaar more about Commander Ziron's subordinates, but knew this wasn't the time. "I know. Thank you, Rejas."

The door slid open to the corridor, and Diego headed out, jogging down the hall toward his cabin. Placing his palm against the identity pad on the door, he waited the few seconds it took for the ship's computer to acknowledge him and report his whereabouts. He flopped onto his bunk. Suddenly a face peered from the bed above him.

Rreengrol grinned. "You were almost late for sleep cycle."

Diego grinned back. He had been wondering which other squire he was sharing a cabin with, and felt lucky to have drawn the Grrlock. "I was with Anaar."

"Told you, didn't I?"

"Yes, and so did Commander Ziron," Diego replied.

Rreengrol's yellow eyes widened. "You told him? You

admitted you couldn't read?"

"I can read," Diego reminded his friend. "But not your language."

Rreengrol laughed a pleasant growling sound. "Those glyphs are not my language either. Ours is based on a fifteen sound alphabet."

Diego pulled out the sheet Anaar had given him and studied it. He frowned. "My language is easier to learn, too," Diego muttered.

The Grrlock laughed again and jumped down from his bunk. "I think mine is easier, as well. Maybe once you learn the Seressin language, we can teach each other our home languages."

"If I can learn all these marks and symbols," Diego muttered.

Rreengrol purred deep in his throat, a sound that indicated feelings of contentment, much like the felines Diego was familiar with at home. The Grrlock sat down beside him and pointed to the first glyph. "That is the sign for star. You add a dot, and it becomes stars. This," Rreengrol said, pointing to another glyph, "is the glyph for ship. If you put them together, it becomes starship."

Diego looked puzzled, and then he brightened. "That is what we are on—a starship."

"Of course."

Diego had not taken time to think about where he was other than it was a great vessel, immensely larger than a galleon. "How can a ship sail from star to star?"

"First of all, we are not sailing, such as I think you are meaning sailing, like on water. A starship uses fuel to push through space. There is a great deal of space between the stars."

Diego thought he understood the concept of fuel, but could not conceive of a great ship like this one somehow using wood to push itself among the stars. "What kind of fuel does our starship use?"

Rreengrol cocked his head, his pointed ears twitching. He looked at Diego with a half grin on his face. "A combination of nuclear fuel and liquid fuels." At Diego's more intensely puzzled face, the Grrlock paused. "There are great gaps in your education. By the way, what kind of transportation did you use on your world, other than sailing boats, that is?"

"Carriages, wagons and horses."

"No wonder you seem backward to the others." Seeing Diego's frown, he continued. "That was not said in offense. I am amazed at how well you have adapted. After you have learned the Seressin written language, you can learn the history of space travel."

"Good. If this is my destiny — out here among the stars — I want to know all there is to know."

"That is a big order."

"I was not born a slave. I will not live as a slave, and I will certainly not die as one," Diego said, a determined glint in his eyes.

Rreengrol's other ear twitched. "I fully believe you, Diego, but it will be hard."

"Yes, I know."

"And you do have friends," the Grrlock assured him.

Diego nodded his gratitude.

"Right now, we'd better get some sleep. I hear squires are

roused early in the morning."

"That's what Marix Ziron said. I guess we should do as the commander wishes."

Rreengrol climbed back up to his bed. After some rustling, it was quiet. The lights dimmed.

Chapter Eight

High above him, the blue vaulted sky seemed to stretch forever. The azure expanse was broken by a tall, white-steepled church on the distant horizon. A bell rang incessantly, first soft like the chimes of little hand bells, and then louder and more strident. Diego jerked up in his bed, still hearing the bells. He wondered where it was coming from in the dark room.

The commander's pin. Diego jerked up his shirt from the end of his bed where he had laid it before sleep overtook him. Throwing it on, he snatched his pants, shoving his legs in as he hopped/raced toward the doorway. He snapped the waistband with one hand as he activated the door mechanism with the other. His shoes were left behind. The door had not fully opened by the time he was in the out of his room. He pounded down the corridor—right, long corridor, left, short corridor, commander's cabin. As he pressed his palm against the door frame, it slid open to the tall, frowning countenance of the commander.

"Fair, but you can do better. In fact, your response will become exemplary." Ziron gazed down at the boy's bare feet. "And in the future, you will be prepared for anything I may require of you when I call." His features were unreadable, and Diego could not tell if the commander was really angry or not.

"Yes, sir," was all he could think of to say.

"You will not know when I will test you again, so you must be ready."

"Yes, Marix."

"You are dismissed. Your schedule of training will be given to you at first meal," Ziron said.

With that, the door slid shut, and Diego was staring at the small command emblem painted on the door. Slowly he turned and walked back to his room, where he quietly slipped into bed. Rreengrol whuffed softly in his sleep and then rolled over and began breathing evenly again.

How can I be ready in the middle of the night? Diego thought. Ideas floated into his brain like wispy clouds, and he finally drifted back to sleep.

***

"Wake up!" a growly voice intruded on half-remembered dreams.

"Leave me alone," Diego mumbled in Spanish.

"You'd better wake up now, or you'll be late for first meal," the voice persisted. It was Rreengrol. Diego opened one eye and glared at his roommate.

"Up, Squire," Rreengrol insisted, pushing him from the narrow bed. Diego hit the floor with a thump.

"Ouch!" he exclaimed, rubbing his shoulder. "Why'd you

do that?"

"You have exactly five micro-cycles to get to the squire's hall for first meal. If you don't, you'll have nothing until mid-meal, which, as you know, is usually late," Rreengrol said.

Taking the Grrlock's outstretched hand, Diego jumped up and dashed to the tiny bathroom. He splashed water on his face, toweled dry, and brushed his teeth. His other hand was grabbing his clothes off the hook at the same time. He threw on his uniform and followed Rreengrol out of their cabin. They reached the squires' dining hall as those at the end of the line were being served.

An emaciated-looking humanoid with parchment-like skin glowered at them. "You almost missed this most glorious of culinary delights. A meal of superb standing," she cackled. She reminded Diego of a witch. He glanced behind her, looking for a cauldron. But instead of noxious brew, she spooned out a kind of sweet, spicy porridge into a bowl where it steamed a fragrant scent. "Eat hearty!" she called out, and then laughed. Even her laughter sounded like what he would imagine a witch's to be, except it was good-natured and happy. Diego found himself grinning even as he sniffed the contents of his bowl. While other slaves had grumbled and complained about the sameness of the morning meal, Diego loved the porridge—the roosh, as they called it here. It was the closest thing to what he had eaten at home that he had in this place.

"Thanks," he said, looking around for a place to sit down. The Treesh from yesterday's class was sitting with another like himself at the only table with any space left. Diego walked over and began to sit down.

"You are not welcome here, mrees," the Treesh growled. Diego remembered Anaar calling this one Hirss.

Irritated, Diego glared at the two grinning Treesh. Then a thought crossed his mind, one he knew could get him in trouble. "You mean right here? This spot?" he asked, pointing to the ground at the Treesh's feet.

"That's right," Hirss declared. "We don't want you here."

Diego saw that the table was not permanently attached to the deck. It was as he guessed. This room had other functions. Turning to Rreengrol, he handed his roommate his bowl and then grabbed the edge of the table. Diego pulled it away from the two surprised Treesh. It wasn't far, as the room was fairly crowded, but it was far enough.

Pulling the two empty chairs to the table, Diego motioned to Rreengrol, took his breakfast, and then sat down. There were a few hoots and gurgles of laughter from other squires, but some watched the Treesh nervously. With a grin, the Grrlock sat next to him and began eating.

The Treesh, their cheek patches orange with rage, began to get up, but a loud voice brought them back to their chairs. Diego shoveled his breakfast down as the barrel-shaped guard from the previous day's last meal stood inside the doorway and bellowed for attention. He didn't have to bellow long. Everyone stopped talking almost immediately. There was only the soft clicking of spoons snatching the last bits of breakfast from bowls.

"Squires, this is your schedule! You will attend to your masters' first meals in five micro-cycles. Then the newly selected squires will continue orientation with Rejas Anaar directly after their masters' first meals. Commanders' mid-meal next, your mid-meals, and martial arts directly following. Free time for thirty micro-cycles, commander's last meal, your last meal, free time, and lights out. That will be your schedule for the next ten cycles." The guard looked around. "You who are older squires will be obliged by honor to assist the new squires if they ask for assistance." He looked around again. "You are dismissed. Oh, and Diego, move the table back."

Diego did as he was told, ignoring the glowering looks of the Treesh. Then he and the others dashed to their respective masters' dining halls.

"You did not win any points with our friends back there," Rreengrol said with a purring chuckle.

"No way to win with them, no matter what I did. If I had done nothing, I would have been considered cowardly."

It was the same back home. If he placated his older brother as his father wanted him to, he was considered weak. If Diego stood up for himself, or worse yet, laid hand on Reynaldo, his older brother immediately told his father. Either way he lost. Diego glanced back at the glowering lizard men following.

"Be careful, soft-skinned mrees," Hirss snarled.

Diego shrugged and walked out of the dining facility behind the largest group of squires. When he arrived at the commanders' dining hall, he went through the same procedure as he had the night before, except there was no drink afterward. This time all went well, and Diego breathed a sigh of relief as he made his way to Rejas Anaar's classroom.

Rreengrol was Hreeshan's squire, and since Hreeshan was a close commander to Ziron, the two young squires were together most of the day. Only during the first orientation phase were they separated. The next several day cycles came and went without incident, and Diego began to think he might survive this life of his. He gained confidence in his newly acquired reading skills. His meal-time duties became routine. So far, Commander Ziron had not called him for any other duties or tests since the late night summons.

"Do not let down your vigilance, my friend," Rreengrol growled softly at him during mid-meal seven days into his training. Most of the time he was vigilant. He had to be. Hirss and his Treesh friend seemed determined to make him look foolish, especially in front of Commander Ziron.

"My after meal drink, Quirlis," the commander ordered, clacking his claws together, indicating impatience.

"Yes, Marix." Diego dashed to the back of the kitchen. He saw the label for Praesean flame juice and grabbed the bottle, hurrying back to the dining hall. Diego poured the dark red liquid into a small glass.

Ziron picked it up and slowly swished the drink. Putting it to his lips, he paused, then jerked it away suddenly. With a roar, the commander flung the glass across the room and without pausing, swung his hand around and slapped Diego to the ground. "Are you trying to poison me?" he shouted.

Diego lay on the floor, staring at his master. "The label...."

Ziron took a brief moment to gaze at the bottle, then turned his yellow-orange eyes to the boy. "The label means nothing. You must check inside the bottle as well as what is outside." He picked up the bottle, and with one claw, easily tore the label off. What was underneath made Diego gasp. It was a meat preparation liquid, something the cooks used to tenderize meat that was tough.

"Yes, Commander." Diego judged it was safe to pick

himself off the floor. He bowed deeply. The Treesh hissed in soft laughter.

"Get rid of this and bring me something fit to drink," Ziron ordered. "And get the right drink, or this time I may not be so gentle."

Bowing again, Diego turned and trotted back to the kitchen. He felt his cheek, chagrined at the lump that was already forming. He checked the bottles of flame juice. Taking one off the shelf, Diego set it on a cabinet and pulled off the seal. He didn't think the Treesh had the ability to tamper with the liquid and then reapply a seal. Pulling out the stopper, Diego sniffed the pungent liquid. That part fit the description. Tipping it, Diego let a drop lay on his finger, then he tasted it, grimacing. It tasted like a bitter herb vinegar.

Putting the stopper back on, the boy dashed back out the door. "Marix, I believe this is right, but...."

"But what?" Ziron demanded, his voice ominous.

Diego tried to ignore the clenching, clawed fist. "I do not know what Praesean flame juice tastes like."

Ziron stared at him for several heartbeats. Then he started to chuckle. Diego held his breath. Ziron's chuckles turned into full-throated laughter. Diego stood silently. Everyone else was silent as well, except for the most senior commanders. They sat with indulgent smiles. Hreeshan made a purring rumble deep in his throat.

"Then let me teach you, Quirlis," Ziron said, pointing to a glass.

Diego poured and handed the drink to the commander.

Ziron took it and sniffed. He gazed at Diego. "You tasted it?"

Diego nodded. "Yes, Marix."

"At least it's not a fatal poison," Ziron said to his subordinates. He put the glass to his hard-scaled, yellowish lips and tasted it. "Ah, yes," he said. "Wonderful vintage." The Seressin finished the drink and motioned for Diego to pour more. "Now you drink it."

Knowing what the taste was like, Diego hesitated, but then he took a swallow. He choked as the vinegary liquid slid down his throat. *Flame juice is right,* Diego thought. His eyes watered, and he began coughing.

"Now you know, Quirlis."

Diego resisted the urge to audibly sigh. The rest of the evening was uneventful, except for his queasy stomach. Finally, the first-year squires were dismissed, and Diego almost ran back to his cabin, where he threw up the offending liquid. It was as bad coming up as it had been going down.

"Feel better?" Rreengrol asked.

"A bit," Diego murmured. He washed his face and drank some water to try and take the taste of the horrible liquid away. He went on to Anaar's classroom, where he learned more glyphs before he went to bed. His stomach was still aching as sleep overtook him.

Chapter Nine

His sleep was filled with nightmares, seemingly set in California on his father's ranch, but with three moons hanging in the sky. One of the moons was dark-red and bloated on the horizon; the other two small and white, chasing each other higher in the sky. Lightning filled the sky from one horizon to the other, brighter, angrier, and more violent than anything Diego had ever seen. The lightning's sharp smell made his eyes water. The thunder raged, deafening and constant. The ground shook, making it hard to stand up straight. A herd of his father's horses came stampeding straight for him, their eyes wide with fright, and their screams almost as loud as the thunder.

Diego looked around wildly, trying to find an escape. Marix Ziron lay nearby, his leg obviously broken. The ground shook again, causing him to stumble. Ziron was saying something, but he could not understand the words. Diego waved his arms, scaring a few of the animals, but most continued toward them. Then a massive lightning bolt struck in the middle of the herd, killing many outright and panicking the rest. They bore down on him.

Fear seized his heart, and he jumped to his feet and ran. He was still running when the frightened animals thundered past him. Just when he thought he was safe, a lone beast knocked him down, one of its hooves stamping down on his arm. He screamed his agony.

Diego woke up to darkness, his heart hammering. *A dream. It was a nightmare.* Realizing it was a dream didn't help him forget that he had abandoned his master. He had run away and left his commander to be killed. Was he a danger to the marix? Rreengrol muttered in his sleep, but was soon making the purring snore sounds of deep sleep.

Diego lay back down and tried to go back to sleep. For a long time he pondered, tossing and turning. Surely he was braver than that. *It was a dream, just a dream!* He kept reminding himself of that even while feeling the guilt of a betrayer. Finally, he fell into a fitful sleep, where he alternately dreamed of riding the rolling hills of his homeland and of crashing thunder and strange landscapes of other worlds.

"Wake up, hibernator," Rreengrol urged, shaking him awake. "If I didn't know better, I'd think you had spent the night walking the corridors."

"I feel like I did. Nightmares."

"The flame juice, I guess," the Grrlock suggested.

Diego sighed and headed for the shower. The day moved with deliberate slowness, thankfully uneventful. His mind felt as though it was mired in a tar pit.

Even Anaar was impatient with him. "Diego, I do believe you have regressed," the android commented. Diego muttered an apology. Anaar finally cut the lesson short.

In martial arts class Diego was paired against Wors, the first year Treesh. The snake-like creature hissed in anticipation, while Diego's heart sank. The weapons were ropes with knobby stones on each end. Diego examined his, trying to think where he had seen something similar. *Bolas*, he thought. He remembered the South Americans who had visited Los Angeles last year. One of them had put on an exhibition with his bolas, easily knocking the head off a practice dummy. When Diego had asked, the gaucho had gladly taught him the rudiments, and had praised him when he gained enough control of them to at least connect with the dummy.

"These are xringas," Hreeshan announced, smiling as he preened his whiskers. "They look benign, but can be quite deadly. It is their seeming innocence that makes them an effective weapon." Hreeshan took the xringas and, grasping the rope almost in the middle, began a swinging cadence that soon had the weapon whistling as it flashed around his head. Suddenly the Grrlock let go, and the xringas sailed through the air, the whistling changing to a shriek that was cut off as the weapon hit the target set up in front of the far wall.

Some of the squires gasped in amazement. Hreeshan's grin widened. "Has anyone ever used these?"

Wors raised his hand. "I have, Rejas," he announced.

Without saying anything, Hreeshan handed the xringas to the Treesh and motioned for everyone to back away. Wors took the weapon and began swinging, not as smoothly as the master, but still well enough for the xringas to whirl in a circle around his head. Suddenly Wors let go, and the end weights flew a short distance before skittering across the floor toward

Diego. Diego danced out of the way, but not quickly enough to avoid getting clipped on one ankle. Stifling a cry of pain, Diego glared at the Treesh.

"There are many ways to incapacitate an enemy," Wors smirked.

"Yes, there are," Hreeshan replied. "But it would appear that more practice is in order before you could consider yourself a master of the xringas, Quirlis Wors," the Grrlock added sarcastically. He turned to Diego. "Would you care to try? With a practice pair, that is."

Diego followed the master's gaze and saw a slightly smaller, more benign pair hanging from the weapon rack on the wall. Trying to recall exactly how Hreeshan had held the xringas, Diego also remembered how he had held the bolas. The practice version of this alien weapon had about the same balance as the earthly ones. He remembered the gaucho's admonitions, and the chuckles from those who didn't think he could do it, including some of his friends. Diego felt there was a bit more at stake now.

He began swinging the xringas above his head. His body moved in cadence to the circular motion of the ropes. As soon as he heard the xringas whistling, he concentrated on the target Hreeshan had aimed at. His problem back home was timing—when to release the weapon. As he continued twirling the xringas, Diego felt his arms, studied the target, and tried to get in sync with the correct time of release.

Now! Diego loosed his grip and let the weapon fly. To his chagrin, the xringas went wide of the target by a foot, clattering against the far wall.

"You did not say you had used xringas before, Quirlis

Diego," Hreeshan said, pride evident in his voice. The two Treesh were flicking their tongues in and out in annoyance.

"I have not, Rejas," Diego replied. "But there are weapons on my home planet called bolas that are similar. I have used them once or twice."

Hreeshan nodded. "You did well, Quirlis." He addressed the group. "Now, pairs work with the practice xringas. Critique one another. I will be judging you all on both your use of the xringas and your partnership cooperation."

In one corner of the room, Diego and Wors stood and glared at each other for a few moments. Finally, Diego sighed and said, "We will not be critiqued well if we don't make some kind of effort to practice."

"I do not need to practice," Wors hissed.

Diego bristled. "So you meant to hit my ankles instead of my head?" Diego asked. "Thanks. I was wondering for a while."

Wors hissed again. "If I had hit you where I had wanted, I would have been dismissed and never had a chance to be Commander Ziron's quirlis."

Diego was taken aback. "So your service to Commander Breesha is only a means to get into someone else's service? What about loyalty?"

Wors glared at him for a moment, his yellow eyes unblinking. "Let us practice," the Treesh finally said.

Diego was grateful for the slight truce. "You go first so I can learn."

Wors nodded and stepped back. He began swinging in a smooth cadence, round and round. There was no jerkiness in his motions. The weighted ends began whistling, and Diego could see intense concentration on the hard features of the lizard-man. With only slight movement of his claws, Wors let go of the weapon. Unerringly, it shot toward the target, a small round circle painted on the front of the stand that had been set up in front of the far wall. With a clatter, the xringas thudded to the right of dead center.

"That was great!" Diego cried, forgetting his animosity in the Treesh's success.

"I did not hit the center," Wors growled.

"Perhaps not, but that was an excellent cast," the boy declared.

Wors gazed at him meaningfully. "So what is your critique?" It almost sounded like a dare.

Diego went through the Treesh's motions in his mind, especially the release. "I am thinking that you leaned slightly sideways as you released. A little bit to the right."

Wors snorted as though Diego had made that up.

"I don't know if that is the reason you did not hit dead center or not. I am giving an honest observation."

The Treesh retrieved his xringas and walked back to the practice area. Again he began the circular motion in a smooth transition from hanging limp to deadly weapon. Wors concentrated on the target, his tongue protruding slightly from between his pointed teeth, his eyes intense. Diego watched carefully. When Wors released the xringas, he saw that the Treesh had compensated. The xringas flew toward the target and hit it straight in the center. Grunting, Wors walked toward the target without saying a word.

"Now that was a terrific throw!" Diego exclaimed.

As he walked back to the practice area, the Treesh simply

said, "Your turn."

Nodding, Diego took up his xringas and balanced them. He began swinging, trying to get the right cadence.

"Use your shoulders. Keep your torso as still as possible," Wors suggested.

Diego concentrated, feeling the sweep of the xringas smoothing out. He heard the whistle of the weights and gazed intently at the target. At the right time, the boy let go. The weapon sailed in a graceful arc, hitting the target halfway between dead center and the left edge. Diego smiled in satisfaction, feeling that he had done better than he hoped.

"Not bad for a beginner," Wors sneered.

Diego opened his mouth with a ready retort and then shut it again. Getting into an argument would serve no purpose right now. He decided to ignore the tone. "Thank you. Your advice helped a great deal."

Wors grunted and said nothing while Diego retrieved his xringas. They practiced a while longer, each giving the other advice, although Diego could find little he could comment on. Grudgingly, he had to admit that Wors was very good with the weapon. At the end of the session, he said as much to the Treesh.

Wors blinked his yellow-gold eyes at him and then said, "I have had much practice." There was a pause. "Were you telling the truth when you said you had not used this kind of weapon much before?"

"Yes. I had the opportunity to try the bolas once before I...was captured," Diego admitted.

"With a little practice, you would be expert. You have a natural ability."

Diego looked at the Treesh in open surprise. Finally he said, "Thank you. You are a good teacher."

"But I am not your friend," Wors snapped.

"It is my understanding that we are to train for battle against common enemies," Diego said, repeating part of one of Anaar's lessons. "War comrades need not be friends, they only need to stand together honorably."

"Yes." Wors turned on his heel and strode across the practice room to his friend, Hirss.

***

That evening Diego lay in his narrow bunk, his eyes staring at the bottom of Rreengrol's bed above him, but not seeing anything but the day's events in the practice room. His body was feeling the effects of total exhaustion, but his mind would not let him sleep.

The Grrlock hung his head down from the top bunk, ears twitching and whiskers flicking forward, evidence of his good humor. "Lights out."

"I know," Diego muttered.

"You have not said enough words to fit into dew claw," Rreengrol quipped. "Did something go wrong during the practice session? What I heard was that you showed up our Treesh friends. Did Wors behave like a pringalla's hind leg?"

Diego had no idea what a pringalla was, but he wasn't in the mood to ask. "No, it went well, actually. Almost like a working truce. But he made it clear that he wanted my position."

"I knew that. He was spitting fire when the word got out that you had been chosen for the commander's squire. And a newly-recruited slave, to boot." Rreengrol swung down from his bunk and sat next to the human. "Be careful. I don't think Wors and his friends will do anything blatant, but they will never stop trying to get a promotion as squires to higher commanders. And that includes Commander Ziron."

"I know, Rreengrol. What I don't understand is why Ziron picked me in the first place. As you have said, it isn't usual."

"I am not sure, but rumor has it that the commander saw you in a vision or dream."

"What? A vision or dream?"

"Yes, the Ssressin are—um, they take great stock in visions and dreams of the future. He believes you were the right choice to be his squire. Personally, I think you are, too." Rreengrol snapped his fingers, and the lights dimmed.

Diego sighed, not liking that added burden. He also remembered last night's nightmare. He wondered what Ziron would think of that dream.

Chapter Ten

Amber fog rolled like a live thing along the ground, curling around Diego's ankles. It felt oily, slippery. He shuddered at the touch of the cloying mist and looked up to see where his master was. At first, he could see no one, just the fog in the foreground and smoke and dust in the distance. Then he heard a clashing of swords, the hiss of laser weapons, shouts and curses of fighting and dying creatures. Diego spun around, trying to locate the battle. Sounds seemed to be coming from everywhere and nowhere. He ran in one direction, the fog trying to suck him back, hold him in place. Then he heard sounds behind him. Swinging around, he saw Commander Ziron fighting several armored creatures. He didn't ask himself how he had gotten so close so quickly. The commander's blade was covered in a thick green ichor. Ziron's armor was stained with the stuff. He had been acquitting himself well, but he, Diego, the commander's squire, should be there with him. Here he was unscathed and watching as the creatures were overcoming his master. Horror welled up as Diego realized he could not move.

The creatures were thin and tall, but the stick-like limbs appeared strong enough to break him in half. The limbs and body were jointed in strange ways, almost like the walking sticks he had occasionally seen back home in California. Commander Ziron was pulled down, and the creatures swarmed over him, chittering their triumph in loud, creaking squeals. Before he fell, his master caught his eyes. Diego had to go help him—it was his duty. But when he tried to pull out his sword, he couldn't make his arm move. When he tried to run toward Commander Ziron, he could not lift his foot from the ground.

The fog wrapped itself tighter around his ankles and worked its way up his legs. It was cold, freezing his legs. He tried harder to move and finally fell forward. The fog wrapped around his arms, climbing his shoulders.

"Commander! Master!" Then his voice constricted, and he couldn't say anything.

"You have betrayed me," Ziron hissed. "You have betrayed—"

Ziron was buried under the insect warriors. Their clacking, hissing, and screeching rose and rose until it beat inside his head. The fog wrapped around his neck and his head, and he couldn't see the terrible scene anymore. All he knew was that he had failed. He had allowed his master to die and had not lifted a finger to help him.

"No! No!"

Diego gasped awake, his chest heaving to suck in air. He was in his cabin, Rreengrol above him, his soft purring telling Diego that his friend was asleep. It had been a nightmare, like the one the night before. This was probably born of that flame juice wine, too. But did it mean anything? Was it foretelling a betrayal? Diego ran his hand through his hair, took a deep breath, and tried to calm down. It had only been a dream. However, it was a dream that had caused the commander to choose him as a squire. Could the reptilian's dream be more powerful? Was Diego's dream more than the effects of something his body couldn't handle? He debated whether he should tell Commander Ziron about his dream. If he did, he might be demoted without even proving himself. *No*, he told himself as he lay back down. *No, it was a dream. It didn't mean a thing.* All he had to do was work hard to be the best squire he could be for his master.

***

Several weeks later, Diego looked at his new uniform critically in the full length mirror. While it appeared almost skin-tight, the material was supposed to be durable and almost impervious to heat and cold. It also was partially protective against many weapons. *Better than armor,* Diego thought. *Armor wasn't anywhere near this comfortable. At least the suit in Father's house didn't look that comfortable.*

The color was a bit garish to his eyes, a bright yellow with wide lavender stripes down each side. The boots were also lavender, soft-soled, and extremely comfortable. On his bunk lay his sword. It was ceremonial and somewhat small, more like a long knife. The blade was sharp and could be used to protect the commander. In the back of his mind he hoped it wouldn't be necessary to use it.

"Ai! By the whiskers of my departed dam! I could wear something like this every day," Rreengrol said, running his hand down his torso. He grinned as he belted on the sword. "Shall we present ourselves for inspection, Diego?"

Diego grinned back. "Yes, I suppose we should." He opened a small drawer in his wardrobe and pulled out a tiny dirk, its blade hidden inside the handle. That slipped in an equally tiny pocket inside the material under one arm. A few other tiny items were hidden in other obscure places.

Rreengrol laughed. "You plan on a battle?"

"I want to be prepared for anything," Diego said seriously.

The cat-man shrugged and finished dressing, and they made their way down the corridor to the embarkation hall. Rreengrol walked over to his master, sub-commander Hreeshan, while Diego stationed himself near Commander Ziron. He stood at attention while one of the sub-commanders in charge of the squires inspected him. With a motion and a nod, the reptilian passed him off.

"We are negotiating with the son of the planetary monarch," Ziron began. His voice echoed in the shuttle bay. His uniform was utilitarian, as theirs was, but with the adornment and weaponry that denoted his rank. Medals shone on his chest, and a silver crusted helmet was under his arm. Diego had polished the equipment yesterday after training. He saw nothing that might make one think less of the service he was giving his master.

"Be ever vigilant," Ziron continued. "These are a cunning people. They wish to be allies, but want as many concessions as they can get. They are also negotiating with the Resh. The Resh would like nothing better than to add the Koressians to their list of comrades in arms."

Diego had not had time to study these Koressians, but

figured he'd meet them soon enough. The Resh, on the other hand, he had studied. They were stockier than the Seressin, but they were no less powerful. Diego had been told that one swipe of a Reshian arm could literally take his head off. The Resh had established themselves in a vast quadrant of the galaxy. Their borders had enlarged a millennia ago to encroach into Seressin territory. Deadly warfare had flared, with several planets being incinerated before negotiations began. The last centuries had been unsettled, but the established truce held. Each mission to an unallied planetary system began with the presentation of a ceremonial diplomatic cylinder that denoted the carrier's assurance of good faith. Since the Resh and the Seressins often were vying for the same planets, the ceremony assured peace.

"This is a good day to conquer!" Ziron ended his speech with the customary Seressin call to duty.

The squires followed their masters into the shuttle. Diego studied the cabin, making sure there was nothing amiss that might harm Commander Ziron. Not that he was sure what might not be normal in the small ship — he'd never been in one before. Rreengrol tapped him on the shoulder and pointed. His master was gazing at him expectantly. There was a hissed snicker in the background. Diego almost jumped the two steps to the commander's side and took the ceremonial sword and diplomatic canister. He stood straight as a rod as Ziron sat down on the flight couch. Then Diego placed the sword in its holder/sheath and sat down on a smaller flight chair behind his master. He buckled the safety harness one-handed while keeping the canister close to his body. It would lay cradled in his lap during the journey. Ziron glanced back at him and made a grunting noise deep in his throat. By now, Diego knew that sound meant the master was satisfied. He let his breath out and relaxed against the soft foam back. While he couldn't nap on the trip down, he would let his body rest. Diego did the exercises that allowed his muscles to relax even while he pulled energy from the special supplements that he and the other squires had eaten earlier in the day. He would be ready for anything, and would not let the commander down.

Diego leaned his head back and recalled the instructions he had received from the computer instructor, Anaar—the protocols, the ceremonies, and the duties he had while they were planet-side. He had barely figured out ship-board protocols, and now he had to remember all the nuances of visiting a strange planet. He relaxed and loosened his muscles until a bump brought him to full alertness. It was the bouncing of the shuttle on the upper reaches of the Koressian atmosphere. Diego was amazed at the ease with which this tiny spaceship shot through space from its mother ship to the ground below. There was a monitor nearby that he watched as the craft went from the blackness of space into velvety purple of the upper atmosphere. He watched waves of heat make the air shimmer in a violet haze at the bow of the shuttle. The darkness was replaced by bright reddish-orange sunlight that made Diego's eyes water. Almost instantly a shade dropped across the monitor. His ears popped as the ship shifted. Diego was now able to see land and water below. The land was a strange amber color. The water was blue green and dotted the land in small, round lakes. Strangely, they all appeared to be the same size and about the same distance apart.

The shuttle shuddered slightly as it came closer to the

planet. He could feel the engines slowing them down. The amber ground defined itself into sandy soil. Short hills rose up on the horizons. Stunted brush and trees showed as the ship touched down on the landing field.

Even before the engines completely cooled, the squires jumped up, holding out their commanders' swords. Ziron took his with almost reverent care.

"Are you ready?" he asked.

Diego was taken by surprise and stammered out. "Yes, sir."

"Good. This will be a difficult mission." Ziron seemed to be saying the last almost to himself.

"You will prevail, Master."

Ziron nodded as he sheathed his sword.

The hatch opened, and two of the sub-commanders stepped down the ramp ahead of Ziron. A delegation of Koressians was waiting near the end of the ramp. As Ziron stepped onto the ramp, Diego saw them clearly, and almost gasped in surprise. They were the creatures of his nightmare; the ones that overpowered his marix while he stood there unable to do anything. Diego almost stumbled, and then he quick-stepped to catch up to Commander Ziron. He had to warn him, but as quickly as he thought that, Diego knew this was not the time. A little later. It didn't appear that the Koress were interested in their ambush right now. Perhaps he could warn the commander after they had gone to their guest quarters.

Diego glanced to each side and saw a line of Koress warriors on either side of the commander's group. He took stock of his hidden weaponry. Of course, as this was a peace mission—the only visible weapons were the ceremonial ones. The Koress had pistols strapped to their multi-jointed thighs and armor to augment their natural body coverings. They stood stiffly, their unblinking eyes impassive. Diego had to repress a shudder.

Commander Ziron gave a soft growl, and Diego remembered the protocol. He handed his rejas the diplomatic cylinder with a bow and moved one step to Ziron's right. His master handed it to a Koress, who was taller than Ziron by at least two feet. The Koressian leader tapped the seal, which caused the top to open. He extracted a small card and put it into a machine his squire was holding in front of him. He gazed at the symbols on the machine's screen. With a clicking noise, the Koressian put the card back into the cylinder and handed it to Ziron.

Ziron growled almost inaudibly and motioned to Diego. The boy stepped forward to take the cylinder, but the insect man would not give it to him. This was not in Anaar's protocol program, and Diego was at a loss to know what to do. Furiously, he thought of what he could do to help his commander save face. "It is the custom that the squire does this duty so that the commander may give his full attention to his illustrious ally." Diego knew that the Koressian was getting an immediate translation. He held his breath. Ziron had made no move.

There was a clicking that translated to satisfaction, and the cylinder was dropped into Diego's waiting hands. He clipped it to his waist and stood at attention.

"You will accompany us to guest accommodations, where you can rest and prepare for the last meal and evening activities," the translation told them.

Diego was elated. That meant he could talk to Commander Ziron privately.

As they walked between the Koressian warriors, Diego noticed several vehicles waiting for them. There were not nearly enough for all of the commander's men, however.

"Your servants will wait for the vehicles to return for them," one of the Koressians told Commander Ziron.

Ziron gave another growl, but this one was audible. "You were told of the number of my retinue. We will wait for additional transportation."

"We are not a wealthy world. This is our best."

"The accommodations do not appear to be that far. We will walk," Ziron said with finality.

"As you wish," the Koressian said.

The sun was low, but still hot and in their eyes. Diego followed several of the group's members and lowered the eye shield goggles. His eyes quit smarting, but the intense heat was brutal. There was nothing in the protocol that allowed him to get a drink while marching in formal processions, so he refrained. Within a short time, however, Diego felt as though his tongue had swollen three times its size and that all the moisture had been sucked out of his body. The building he had seen in the distance didn't seem to be coming any closer. If anything it wavered farther away. *How could that be,* he wondered? Sweat rolled down his back, and his sleek uniform chafed.

He felt his feet dragging and concentrated on continuing the pace the Koressians had set. A quick motion from Ziron told Diego that his unsteadiness had been noticed and was not acceptable. Diego picked up his feet and tried to keep from bringing shame to his master.

Finally they arrived at the building that would house them for the duration of their stay on Koress. It was cooler, and there was moisture in the air. Diego stumbled over the threshold, and Ziron's iron-clawed grip almost made him cry out in pain. He bit his lip and stood straighter. Only when they were in their private quarters did anyone say anything.

"Perhaps I was wrong to think you were determined."

"Marix, I...."

"No excuses. However, when we return to the ship, we will have the medical staff determine which atmospheres might be detrimental to you," Ziron told him.

"Sir, there is something I must tell you," Diego began.

"There is no time. We are to meet for last meal before the setting of the sun. Their stunt with the vehicles has put us behind."

Diego felt desperation clawing in his chest. "Marix, I think there is something wrong going on."

"And you base that on what?"

How could he tell his master that he had had a dream? Even though Ziron had supposedly had a dream about him, Diego didn't know how to voice his suspicions. "I...it's a feeling, sir. I have—"

"No time. I have unease as well, but if we are vigilant—" There was a chime at the door. "Hurry!"

Before he opened the door, he tried one last appeal. "Rejas, I had a dream."

Ziron stood rigid for a second before turning to his squire. "About?"

"The Koressians, sir. They will try to ki…harm you or capture you." Diego still couldn't admit his part in the dream.

"It is too late to back away from this now. We will watch each other's backs. Tonight you will tell me more about this dream." At Diego's nod, he continued. "Answer the door."

Chapter Eleven

It was Moreeng and Phoril's rejas, Soloy and Thris. The set of the Seressins' mouths showed their displeasure, but Soloy didn't say anything other than, "We are expected."

Moreeng, a burly mammalian with a rat-like face, looked uncomfortable, but not anxious. They glanced at each other as their commanders left the room, but Diego was unable to say anything to his fellow squires. He mouthed the word, "Watch." Phoril's whiskers twitched in acknowledgement. He was a distant cousin to Rreengrol, but with little of his relative's imagination and sense of adventure.

They followed their leaders down a narrow corridor that appeared almost cave-like. There were decorations painted on the wall, but they were geometric, showing squares, hexagons, and triangles touching each other and partly covering other designs. Lights set high in the ceiling made long shadows when they passed beneath them. Diego was aware of the guards behind them chittering to each other, but there was no translator so he had no idea what they were saying to one another. Guards at the far door opened it up as the group approached.

"The evening winds herald the evening meal amongst our people," a Koressian said with a bow, indicating a tall table at the end of the room. "Please make yourselves comfortable."

Diego gazed at the table and chairs in dismay. The spindly stools would not hold a Seressin's weight. It would seem that the Koressians were trying to antagonize Commander Ziron.

"We regret that your chairs will not hold one of our kind," Soloy, Phoril's rejas, replied. "Do you have anything of more substance?" he asked with barely concealed sarcasm.

"We are sorry, Commanders, that we do not have any such things," the insect man said with a bow. "Our heads hang with shame, and the architects of this meeting will pay the price of their oversight."

"That is not necessary. We will stand." Thris, Moreeng's rejas, made a slight gesture that was an indication of his irritation. If the Koressian understood what it was, it didn't react. The squires were conducted to a separate table behind a partition.

"Rejas...," Diego began, worried about his master.

Ziron shook his head.

"I don't like it," Diego whispered to his companion as they followed the Koressian guard.

"Neither do I, but what can we do?"

"I guess be vigilant."

"You already are. You have been as nervous as a fellek beetle on ice. Is there something I should know?" Phoril asked.

"I had a dream," Diego replied, not sure why he suddenly confided in these two. They were not close, but he had no reason to distrust them, especially Phoril.

"You, too? No wonder the commander likes you."

Diego nodded. "They are going to try to do something, but exactly what or how is unknown to me. What do you think we should do?"

"Listen and wait. There is nothing we can do other than that."

"I can sneak to the back and try to hear what some of them are talking about."

"You don't have a clue how to get around in this warren," Moreeng pointed out.

Before Diego could say anything else, several Koressian servers brought out food in steaming bowls. The squires studied their food, which looked to Diego to be chunks of beef in a strange-colored gravy. The greenish brown hue of the gravy was bad enough, but the fact that the chunks of meat looked like they were moving on their own added to the weirdness of the meal.

"Your food has been tested and found compatible with your digestive systems," the server informed them. "This is a delicacy on our world. Makavian cave fish soup."

"Is it alive?" Phoril asked, poking the contents of the bowl with his spoon. The chunk bobbed and then continued to swim around the container.

"It has been cooked, young squires. The motion you see is that of chemical reactions to the preparation. It is safe to eat."

Moreeng scooped up a small amount in his spoon and tasted a few drops of the broth. He straightened up with a surprised look on his face. "Not bad," he declared.

Diego tried a spoonful of his and found the taste a bit

spicy, but not unlike what the cook used to prepare back on the hacienda. He took another bite and then another. "You're right, it's quite good."

The servers bowed and left the room. Diego and his friends finished their meal and sat back contentedly. The bowl of soup was filling as well as delicious.

A Koressian walked up to their table. His garb was different than that of the guards. The alien bowed. "Your masters wish your presence at this time," he intoned in heavily accented words.

"About time," muttered Diego.

The Koressian did not lead them out the same way they had arrived. Diego felt something tingle between his shoulder blades and looked over his shoulder. Several Koressians had fallen in behind them with weapons drawn. They were not guards, at least not the ones they had seen before. These had painted their bodies in a garish combinations of green, purple, and yellow that made them seem even more threatening than the armored guards. They wore turban-like headdresses and wrappings around their torsos. While their garb, or lack of it, might have made some think these creatures were not capable warriors, Diego knew they were deadly. They were also out to kill them.

"Phoril! Moreeng! Watch out!"

Diego pulled out his less than effective sword to engage the first creature, but it was sliced in two at the Koressian's first blow. Fear froze his limbs as he saw the ease of the warrior's blow. Phoril's howling scream told Diego that the other squire was not doing any better. Blaring horns and bells reverberated in his skull. The creatures rushed him, and all

Diego could do was to dodge out of their way. He tried to trip one of them, but the Koressian grabbed his shoulder, the steel-strong fingers digging into his flesh. Diego clutched the bony wrist and tried to wrench the warrior's hand away, but was no more successful in that as he had been with his sword. Pain surged down his arm and side, and he dropped to his knees. He heard a scream and realized it was his voice. The creature threw him across the hallway, and Diego's head hit the wall with a resounding thump. He slid down the wall, dazed, but not completely knocked out. His eyes didn't seem to be working, and he called out for his companions.

Another bony hand jerked him up, and he was dragged along the corridor. The blaring continued. There was another noise. Diego couldn't figure it out, but the creature dropped him. There was more chittering, but it faded from the squire's consciousness.

Chapter Twelve

Diego woke to soft beeps and chirps, a cacophony of odors, and a gentle vibration under his back. Diego realized he was back on the ship, but where?

Commander Ziron! He tried to sit up, but a sharp lancing pain in his head forced him back down. A hand was also pushing against his chest, that of an unfamiliar Seressin in med bay garb. So this was the med bay. But then Diego realized this was not the same place he had been in before. Still, his first concern was his rejas.

"You are in no shape to fight any battles now," the Seressin told him.

"Commander Ziron? Is he all right?"

"He negotiates with the Koressians."

"Koressians attacked us. Moreeng and Phoril.... They were different than the guards. They were like wild men."

"Moreeng and Phoril were killed in the attack, as was the Koressian guard who was with you."

"They are dead?" Diego automatically made the sign of

the cross. He had not known them that well, but they had been good comrades. Anger warred with sadness. Anger won. They had been led into an ambush. "The Koressian guard disappeared at the time the strange warriors appeared. Their weapons sliced through our swords like a hot knife through cullis pudding," he explained.

"That is not what the vid-file showed," another voice said.

Diego turned his head too quickly and felt a stabbing pain down his neck. "Who...who are you?"

The speaker was a thin-boned Seressin, a little taller than his rejas. "I am Gorlis, the ship's legal counsel."

"Huh? Uh, why are you here?"

"You."

"Me? What did I do? And what do you mean about a vid-file? Is that a computer teacher like Anaar?"

Gorlis shook his head. "No, it is a record of things that have happened. This particular vid-file is what happened during your so-called attack."

"So-called? We *were* attacked!"

"According to the record, you defied the guard and ran away from him before the desert fighters attacked. You were injured when other guards found and subdued you."

Diego closed his eyes and tried to remember what had happened. They had been separated from the commanders. He told Gorlis that, and then told him everything that happened up to the time he lost consciousness. "I swear it by the Holy Mother of God. I would swear it before the pope," he ended fervently.

"Hmm," was all Gorlis said.

He handed Diego a box that resembled Anaar, but was

smaller. When the box was activated, Diego saw all the events that Gorlis had said and more. According to the vid-file, the warriors had come in through a door Diego had left open. How could he have missed these desert fighters if they were on the other side of the door? He suggested as much. "I don't understand. How can a teaching box—uh, vid-file—show things that aren't true? It didn't happen that way. I didn't run away. I tried to get away from the strange warrior who was attacking me, but I wouldn't abandon Moreeng and Phoril. I wouldn't...."

Gorlis looked thoughtful. "Perhaps this has been tampered with or altered, but the truth of the matter is that it will be hard to prove since this is a copy of the original vid-file. The Koressians are demanding your return to the planet so they can execute you for the death of the guard."

Diego felt the blood drain from his face. "But how could I have killed him when he wasn't even in the room with us?" he asked.

"They are saying you caused his death by desertion and by allowing the marauders access to the facility. The bodies were all together in that corridor, ours and their guard. All had been murdered by these warriors. What is even worse is that the royal guard died after saying you had run away."

"I didn't, Rejas! I swear it."

Gorlis tapped a button on his comm. "I will continue to study this, even as the commander strives to save your life." The counsel left Diego with his thoughts.

A shape detached itself from a shadowy corner of the medical bay and padded over to the young squire. It was Rreengrol. Phoril was his cousin, so he wouldn't blame him if he was angry. "I'm sorry, Rreengrol."

"I am too, Diego."

He couldn't read his roommate's face, couldn't tell his emotions. "I didn't abandon them, Rreengrol."

"I heard."

"You believe me, don't you?"

Rreengrol grabbed his shoulder, and Diego made a soft cry despite himself. It was the shoulder the desert fighter had gripped and had seemingly been trying to rip off. The squire's claws unsheathed, and their tips dug into Diego's skin just enough to draw blood. Rreengrol released him and stared at the red droplets that oozed from the pricks. One claw gathered the blood and raised it to a slightly protruding tongue.

Diego knew that Rreengrol was doing something peculiar to his own kind's customs, so he said nothing. The shoulder throbbed, and Diego continued to watch his roommate. Rreengrol closed his eyes, his tongue still sticking out from between his jaws. The whiskers twitched, and there was a slight purring rumble deep in the squire's throat. After what seemed an eternity, the tongue disappeared, and the rumble grew louder.

Finally, Rreengrol's green eyes slitted open, and he studied Diego. "You speak the truth, as I felt you would."

"What did you do? Or can I ask that?"

"In our culture, the life fluid can never lie. Our people have the ability to taste the blood of another and tell if truth is in the individual."

It was good to be believed by someone. "Thanks, Rreengrol." Then he thought of something. "If I supposedly ran away, how would my sword have been broken?"

"You mean this one?" Rreengrol asked.

Diego gazed at the unblemished sword in his roommate's hand. "No, I saw that fighter slice my sword in two. And it was quite easy for him to do. Can I see that?" Rreengrol handed it over. Diego turned it over and examined the place where his sword had been damaged. This sword showed no evidence of being broken. It was too bad the squires' ceremonial swords were all the same and not considered possessions of the wearer. He would have given anything right now to have had his mark on the hilt. "This can't be my sword."

"There were two broken swords at the place where our comrades were found dead."

"One of those is mine, Rreengrol."

"I believe you, but now the problem is how to get those swords back."

"Aren't they with the bodies when they are sent to the warrior world?"

Rreengrol purred softly in this throat before giving Diego a toothy grin. "You are indeed a smart human. I will speak with my rejas. I believe he will listen to me."

Diego's neck wasn't hurting as much as before. He looked around the small and dimly lit room. "Where is this?"

"Slave's quarter medical bay. You have been banished here for cowardice." Rreengrol shook his head. "You are anything but a coward."

"If I have done so badly, then why not give me to the Koressians and let them execute me? I think I would rather do that than spend my life working the depths of the ship."

"I suspect that something makes Commander Ziron think

there is more to this than what he saw on the vid-file."

"He thinks I might be telling the truth?"

"If not that, he thinks the Koressians are trying to do something against us," Rreengrol assured him. "Do not worry, my friend and comrade, I will not give up on you either. I must go, though, and report to my master. The other squires are doing the same."

"Thanks, Rreengrol. You are a great friend."

"You are, too. And besides, I do not wish to break in another roommate." He grinned.

When Rreengrol left, the med-bay doctor returned. "As soon as I check you over, you will be taken to your new quarters, Quirlis."

"Yes, Rejas," Diego said, much subdued since his friend left.

His guide was a small being much like Phris, but this creature looked almost shrunken on itself. It scuttled along with shoulders hunched and head perpetually bowed. The smells of the working decks were almost overwhelming after living in the squires' quarters. Lubricants, refuse, waste, and all sorts of foul odors lingered and wafted through the corridors. Diego's eyes watered at the pungent smell of overheated electronics mingled with the waste of a variety of beings.

"Hurry, hurry," the creature squeaked.

They padded along corridors that were kept clean of debris but were still grimy. The lighting was much dimmer than what he had become accustomed to in the command part of the ship.

"Here, here. This is your place to sleep."

The place was a cramped room with bunks, hammocks, and nests crammed into any space available. "Which one is mine?" Diego asked.

"Yours? You have to find a space to sleep during your rest rotation," the creature told him. Its voice was almost condescending, like Diego should have known all of this.

"Blankets? Materials to make a bed?" Diego asked, not expecting much.

His guide shook with squeaking laughter. "Where do you think you are, slave? You find your own, fight for it, or barter for it." The creature looked him over. "Perhaps you can fight for a blanket. Certainly nothing to barter." It started to leave.

"Wait a minute," Diego called, irritation coloring his voice. "What do I do other than sleep? What are my duties?"

"Your duties are whatever Master desires you to do."

"Who is my master?"

"Lurin." It started away again.

"You are going to take me to Lurin?"

The squeaks turned indignant. "Was told to show you where you sleep, not to give you tour."

"I have never been down here before. I don't know my way around," Diego explained. "How can I do my duty if I don't know where or what it is?"

"Hmph. Duty? That is funny. Come then. Hurry, hurry!"

They traversed narrow corridors and climbed up ladders. Diego became hopelessly turned around. The creature showed him another ladder and pointed down. "Lurin down there." This time it scuttled away before Diego could say anything.

The ladder led down into a pit that was tinged orange. With a sigh, he began climbing down the sometimes slippery ladder. *What would happen,* he wondered, *if someone else wanted to come up?*

Diego soon found out. A monstrously large Seressin appeared in the haze, clumping up the ladder, making it wobble and shudder dangerously. Diego was unsure what to do—go up or try to let the rejas pass by. Realizing it would be impossible to do the latter, Diego grabbed the rung above him.

At about that time, the Seressin realized there was something above him. Looking up, he roared, "What are you doing here?!" Even the voice shook the ladder.

"I was directed here, Rejas. I was told Lurin was down this ladder, and I was coming to find out what my duties were."

"You have pretty manners for a slave," the Seressin growled. "Get on up, or let go so I can pass."

"Yes, sir," Diego replied, climbing up the grime smeared ladder as fast as he could. Even as large as he was, the Seressin easily kept up with him.

By the time he had pulled himself out of the ladder well, the Seressin was sitting on the edge studying him. Diego tried to regain his breath with as much dignity as he could. He dipped his head in submissive acknowledgment.

"I am Lurin, but never have I requested a new slave to come into my quarters."

"I'm sorry, Rejas. I wasn't told those were your quarters; only that you were there when I asked about my duty station."

"You must be more specific with some of these lesser creatures." He peered more closely at Diego. "What are you?"

"I am human, sir, from Earth."

"What is your name?"

Diego told him.

The golden reptilian eyes widened. "Ziron's squire?"

"I doubt I am his squire any longer."

"If half of what I have heard is true, you are right. You seem a bit on the scrawny side to be a squire to a Seressin commander anyway. I can't imagine why he chose to negotiate for your life rather than handing you over to them. If I had been in his gauntlets, I'd have skewered you right then and there for deserting your comrades," Lurin said.

"But I didn't desert anyone. We were attacked. If anyone deserted, it was that guard who was taking us to our masters. I was framed, and now the Koressians are going to try and kill Commander Ziron."

Lurin growled and cocked his fist. "You talk too much."

Diego expected to have his nose smashed, but as suddenly as the Seressin had threatened him, he calmed down.

"You do not have the temperament of a coward, and that will serve you well here. But you need to keep your thoughts to yourself. Doesn't pay down here to speak your mind. You are here to work, so come with me."

Diego didn't think it wise to point out that he was simply telling the truth. He followed the big Seressin down a corridor and into a room about the size of the training room. Machines lined one wall and most of the other, with a computer station in one corner.

"This is part of the air regeneration station," Lurin pointed out. "You have to monitor the read-outs on the computer and notify the section chief of any abnormalities. You also have to check in every three cycles."

"What are the levels that are normal, Rejas?"

Lurin showed Diego a place on the computer where he could learn about the air regeneration system. It wasn't difficult, despite the fact that his study of the written Seressin language wasn't complete. The hardest part of his job was staying awake, not getting bored. "How long do I serve here?" Diego asked.

Lurin grunted. "Tired of being here already, boy?"

"No, sir, I was curious."

"That can be dangerous, too. Your relief will be here in eight hours. You will give him the last print-out the machine has given you and then go sleep. Brembil showed you your sleeping room?"

"Yes, Rejas." What Diego didn't tell him was that he didn't think there was a chance he could figure out where it was. He figured he could ask the slave who relieved him.

"Good. I have given you a simple task. Do it well, and you'll survive down here."

"Yes, Lurin." Diego figured he might have easily meant that if he did his job well, they would all survive.

After Lurin left, he looked over the tutorial again. That was not the only tutorial. There were places where he could learn other things. Diego began skimming through the index of other topics. He was amazed at how much he was lacking in this life that had been chosen for him. There were lessons in everything from other languages to repairing a variety of machines onboard a ship like this one.

Diego caught himself forgetting the read outs as he focused on other things inside this computer. He barely made the three cycle limit during one of this computer explorations. As he explored the digital library, Diego trained himself to check the monitors at regular intervals. He had gone through four tutorials by the time the slave relieving him arrived.

His replacement was a creature that slightly resembled a Koressian in that it was slender limbed. However, Reelz, the name his replacement gave upon arriving, was shorter and without the insect-like conformation that Koressians had. Reelz was sinuous in his movements, graceful like the best dancers from Diego's homeland. His skin was smooth and slightly moist, while the Koressians had hard, dry skin. Reelz also gave great directions. Diego had no problem getting back to the sleeping area.

Most of the beds were claimed, but there were several that were not. Upon inquiring, he found out that their usual occupants were on their work shifts. He was warned the others would not be happy that someone else had slept in their beds, but Diego wasn't going to worry about it right now. He was too tired to try and find materials to make a bed and then find a place to put it tonight. Despite the unfamiliar and sometimes loud noises, he quickly fell asleep in the hammock he had claimed.

He was awakened when someone jerked him from his bed and threw him to the deck.

"Who said you could sleep in my bed?" the slave bellowed.

Other slaves looked at him and shook their heads, as though Diego was already dead. The angry slave appeared to be of the same stock as Wors, but older.

"You weren't here. I didn't have a bed, and figured by the time you were done with your shift, I'd be getting up," Diego said calmly as he stood up and brushed himself off.

"This is my bed. No one else will touch it!"

He swung at Diego, but the young man was ready. His time training to be a squire was not in vain. Diego leaped close and grabbed the outstretched arm, using the bully's weight against him. Soon the reptilian was flat on his back, looking dazed. With an angry hiss, he jumped up and charged Diego. All the others had backed away, giving the reptilian plenty of room. Diego jerked to the side and swung his leg, kicking his attacker just below the knee. He followed with a leap and a kick to his opponent's stomach. Diego felt pain messages up his leg, but it was minor to what the bully was feeling. With a whoosh, the reptilian collapsed to the deck, trying to suck in air.

"Are you ready to negotiate a truce?" Diego asked quietly. The other wheezed a "Yes."

"Good. I am not interested in fighting. We have enough to worry about down here. I promise I will not take your sleeping area away from you, but if you are on duty and I am tired, I will sleep in this hammock. If you ever lay hands on me again, I will jerk your arm out of its socket," Diego threatened. "Do you understand?" He stood over his attacker, who had not tried to get up yet.

"Yes, I understand, but you had better watch your back."

"And you'd better watch your front," Diego retorted.

His opponent stared at him from the deck. He made a slight choking sound.

When the reptilian didn't make any other move, Diego turned away. "Where do we go to get our meals?" he asked one of the others.

Chapter Thirteen

"I'll take you," a smaller being with an otter shaped head and sleek fur told him. His guide headed down the corridor at a brisk walk. He looked behind to make sure Diego was following him. "You certainly let Jesk have a taste of his own medicine." The speech had a slight lisping quality that Diego had to listen to intently in order to understand.

"He does that to everyone?"

"No, unless they do something to annoy him." That statement was followed by breathy laughter.

Diego instantly liked this bouncy, exuberant creature. "Who are you?"

"Bress. You are the one that was demoted, aren't you?"

"Yes. I was a squire."

"I'm sorry, but Commander Ziron must have liked you a little."

"Why do you say that?"

"Because he didn't kill you outright."

"He's killed squires before?"

"In his younger days, he killed sub-commanders he thought were not good enough. What's a squire compared to a commander?"

Diego shook his head. He didn't really understand it either. Again, he wondered about the treaty. If Ziron wanted to seal a treaty or partnership with the Koressians, why hadn't the commander handed him over and been done with it?

Bress took him through several hatches, up a ladder and down a large corridor to a dim eating area. The aromas that wafted from the kitchen were not as enticing as what he had smelled in the squires' mess, but his stomach still growled. That Koressian meal was the last he had eaten, and it had been a while since that one.

Bress pointed toward the eating utensils, and Diego grabbed a bowl and spoon. As usual, they had the local equivalent of corn porridge that he had been accustomed to eating back on the rancho. He added fruit and sweetener and headed toward an empty table.

"No, over there," Bress pointed out. There were several others like the little otter-man at a table on the other side of the room.

"You sure they won't mind?"

"Oh, no. My brothers and sisters would love to meet you."

"They are your family?"

"Big family!" Bress boasted. "Mother is very hardy."

"So you were captured as a family? At the same time?"

"No, born on the ship. I am from the next to last litter."

So Bress's kind procreated like cats or dogs. "How many are in your family?" Diego asked, his curiosity piqued.

Bress's brow furrowed. "Have to think."

"And aren't you going to have breakfast?"

"Oh, yes! Almost forgot." Bress dashed back to the serving line, grabbed a bowl, and had the server pour some kind of soup into it. Diego could have sworn he saw a fish head in the mixture.

"Two hundred eighty four."

"Two hundred eighty four what?" Diego asked, still wondering what his new friend had in his bowl. "Oh! That's how many are in your family?"

"Yes!" Bress crowed, puffing out his chest.

Diego could understand why Bress was in the communal sleeping room with a family that large. He could also see how a master would love to capture a pair like Bress's mother and father. Slaves without effort. The members of Bress's family who were in the eating room gazed at him, twenty-two pairs of dark eyes staring intently at him. It was disconcerting, like they were trying to see inside of him. Then they all smiled as though they had come to the same conclusion at the same time.

"Welcome, Diego," one of them said. "You are different outside, but inside is the same. I am Writh, this is Preng, Morz, Wreen...."

The list went on and on. Diego knew he would be unable to remember all the names. Then he wondered how they knew his name. Only Bress had known before coming up here. He hesitated at the sudden thought that these people might be telepathic.

Bress beamed at him. "Yes, we understand some thoughts, but we do not try to listen unless it is important."

Diego couldn't help it; he grinned back at the group. He

pulled up a chair and squeezed in with the friendly family. They chattered so fast he couldn't keep up with them most of the time, but he enjoyed the feeling of being part of a family group. He found out that these creatures were called Turengen, and came from a planet that was mostly covered in water.

Diego wondered how they could live in such a sterile place as a spaceship when they had grown up around so much water. Then he remembered that they were telepathic and put a clamp on his thoughts. If they had picked up on what he was thinking, none of them chose to say anything.

Bress showed him around the lower slave area, warning him of places they were not allowed to go. Diego understood that the Seressin equivalent of F through H decks were the places where they worked and lived, and anything above that was forbidden. As squire, he had lived on kang, or C deck. At the time, he had not realized the significance of that designation. Even within his new area, there were places where he was not allowed. The slave work masters' quarters were some of those places. No wonder Lurin had been so irritated.

Later, during his next shift, he reflected that being with Bress's family was a more comforting belonging than he had had with his own kin. His father had been remote, happy to be out buying breeding stock and checking his lands. His mother had been sick a lot, and his brother condescending and arrogant. The vaqueros had been friendly, and were more like brothers than his real brother had been. His little sister was the warmer and more caring member of his family. He wondered how she was doing.

A beeping on the computer screen brought him back to the present. Something kept flashing on the corner of the screen. Diego leaned forward and tried to make out the blinking symbol.

"Come on, Diego. Click on me!"

Diego jerked back when he heard the tinny voice. It sounded familiar, but he wasn't sure because the sound was distorted. Was it a trap, something to get him into more trouble? Then he shrugged. How could he be in worse trouble?

Diego used his pointer and clicked on the little symbol. Just before he clicked, he realized the icon was a cat's head.

"About time," the cat's head said more distinctly. It was Rreengrol's voice.

"Rreengrol?" he asked uncertainly.

"Indeed it is," his friend answered. The cat winked.

"How are you doing this?"

"You have to know how to work these programs."

Diego grunted. "Never heard of anything that would allow people to talk between computers."

"This is a more secure program than typing words back and forth."

"Oh. Didn't know about that, either."

The cat enlarged until it filled a quarter of the screen, and then it smirked at him. "Your education is lacking, my friend. We'll have to rectify that when you are back in the squire's quarters."

"What makes you think that's going to happen?"

The cat face made a soft growl. "It has to happen."

"Why?" Diego asked, worried.

"Because that Wors is insufferable." The face's frown

deepened. Even the whiskers drooped. "And because you are probably the best squire Commander Ziron has had. He and I and my rejas seem to be the only ones who believe that."

"So how do I get out of here?" Diego glanced at the time. "Wait a minute. I have to send in my report."

"I was told you were stuck monitoring the air regeneration system. Better do a good job." The whiskers wiggled. "If you click the face, it will minimize. When you are ready to get back to our conversation, then click it again. Don't take too long. I have some information to give you."

Diego was back talking to Rreengrol in less than a minute. "What's going on?" he asked.

"I think the Koressians are up to something. Probably with the Resh, but that is speculation."

"I already figured that," Diego replied. "And it stands to reason the Resh might be behind it." He recalled some of his history from back home. Governments were always plotting, creating and breaking alliances at the drop of a hat. "So what is going on with the commanders? We hear less than rumor here."

"That is why I wanted to create a secure link when I found out what your duty station was. Not bad for a demoted squire."

Diego wondered about that, too. He would have thought they might toss him farther down cleaning waste or something even nastier. "So what is going on?" he repeated.

"Events and snippets of negotiations. It's almost like they are stalling for some reason."

"Maybe they are still wanting my hide."

"I don't know. I don't think so. Maybe they are satisfied

that you are now the slimiest of the slime on a ship that runs by slave labor."

Diego frowned. As much as he admired Commander Ziron, his leader still supported a system where some beings belonged to others. He pulled himself back to the conversation. "So what are they doing?"

"Well, today we viewed one of their illustrious manufacturing plants, and waited while Commanders Hreeshan, Ziron, Korin, and Mraun negotiated. That didn't even last long enough to have a decent catnap. Then we were wined and dined again; or rather they were. They fed us away from the commanders, and since that ambush you went through, we have brought some of our own rations."

That startled Diego. "Do you think we were poisoned or drugged?"

"The medic wouldn't answer a lowly squire's questions, but that is pretty much what a few of us are thinking. Even Wors is leaning that way. We don't want to take any chances. On our last visit to the ship, we stocked up on basic rations we could hide in our uniforms."

"Hope you also were able to take some kind of weapon. Just in case, mind you."

"Commander Hreeshan gave me permission to bring my personal laser, and the others felt impelled to follow suit."

Diego nodded. "Good! So what else is going on?"

"Basically, each day is about the same as yesterday. I keep trying to figure out what they are planning. I do know that they keep talking about a possible alliance, but the gossip is that Commander Ziron wants to get more concessions."

Diego frowned. They were missing something. "What

happens when there is an alliance made between the Seressin and another race?" he asked.

"Usually at least one high commander comes out for all the official stuff. Sometimes two. Koress is a pretty strategic planet, and that makes it rather important to the Seressins."

"High commander? You mean there are others above Commander Ziron?"

The cat face laughed. "You didn't think the supreme commander would be floating around the space lanes talking with frontier planetary leaders, did you?"

"To be honest with you, I didn't think about it at all. I wanted to know everything about being a squire and ship life, and didn't do more than glance at the disks about Seressin government."

"The supreme commander rules from the home planet. Then there are about ten to twenty high commanders. The number fluctuates. Anyway, they rule over quadrants of the Seressin Empire. There are any number of commanders under the high commanders. Commander Ziron is gossiped to be next in line for a high commander position."

"And if there was a high commander as well as a commander in line to become a high commander...." Diego left the thought unfinished. "But if there are that many high commanders, the loss of one or two wouldn't be that big an issue for the supreme commander, would it? Except to make him extremely angry."

This time it was the cat face that looked perplexed. A little paw smacked the icon in the forehead. "Of course!"

"What?"

"You are brilliant for a backwoods frontier planetary low-life human!" Rreengrol exclaimed.

"Thanks. I think. What did I do?"

"There is a reason Commander Ziron is in line for high command."

"Other than the fact that he is supposed to be a brilliant commander?"

"He is a possible successor to the supreme commander someday." The cat face went through a myriad of emotions. "If the high commander most likely to come out for this—who is Ziron's uncle, by the way, and an heir to the supreme command—were killed at the same time, that would make for a chaotic time on the home planet. Other worlds might try to rebel in the confusion that followed." The symbol looked a little angry, then it calmed. "Of course, I am conjecturing, and I am a lowly squire."

"I think you are on the right track, Rreengrol. So what do we do?" Diego asked.

"You do nothing for the time being. I may try to feel Commanders Grell and Hreeshan out and let them know our concerns. They may already have thought of this, and that's why they are stalling for concessions." Rreengrol sighed. "I had better head to bed before someone wonders why I am spending so much of my sleep time playing computer games."

"How can I contact you?"

"You can't. I know your schedule, and I'll get with you. I'll let you know what has happened each day."

"Okay. By the way, do you know why the commander didn't simply hand me over to the Koressians? It would have made negotiations easier for him if he had."

"I just told you how intelligent you are, and you ask a

question like that?" Rreengrol asked. "Bonehead, he likes you!" And his friend cut the connection.

Ziron had a funny way of showing his fondness, Diego thought with a wry smile. He continued his shift thinking about what Rreengrol had told him. It frustrated him that he was stuck in the bowels of the ship when he wanted to be at his master's side protecting him. Not knowing what else to do, Diego studied more tutorials. Most of them dealt with the Resh; their history, their government. He thought it curious that they and the Seressin were somewhat similar to one another, but none of the experts believed there was any bio-historical common ground. He mentally shrugged and continued with his studies.

After his sleep cycle, he prowled permitted areas with Bress and several of his relatives. Besides the regeneration plants, there were the hydroponics areas. Diego was fascinated with the way plants could grow with no soil. He was not so fascinated with the algae based soup that bubbled in several huge vats. Certainly, he didn't want to know that much of their food was based on that mixture.

"Bress, what would happen if there was an accident on board the ship?" Diego asked his friend. "How would the crew escape?"

"Suspect not everyone would, friend Diego."

"You mean there is no way out for the slaves?" he asked with a frown.

"Did not say that, but I do not believe there are enough escape shuttles for us down here," Bress explained, and ruffled his fur in a sign of resignation.

"Where are these shuttles?" Perhaps the main reason

most of them would not escape was because no one told the slaves where they needed to go if there was some kind of emergency.

"Many are not told, but Bress and his family know where they all are. We are small and not noticed. We are also the ones that do jobs in tight places. Shuttle systems are very little."

A thought entered Diego's mind, and he eagerly followed Bress. When his friend showed him the first shuttle, he noted the level and position of the escape hatch. "This one is the closest to our quarters?"

"Yes, but there are others not too far away. They have about five in each escape bay. The bays are built at intervals inside the outer hull."

Bress showed him several more before they headed off to the food hall. Diego mused while Bress's family talked all around him.

On the next shift, Diego waited eagerly for Rreengrol to contact him. It didn't happen until near the end of the shift. "About time you got a hold of me," he said to the cat head.

"The commanders had me running all sorts of errands. Can't talk long. I wanted to tell you that we'll be away from the planet-side base for a few days. I'm not going to take a chance doing this on a common computer."

Diego was disappointed, but totally understood. "Have you found out anything else?"

The little cat shook its head. "Not really. Mostly gossip."

"Tell me the gossip, then."

"The supreme commander is getting impatient, and wants Commander Ziron to work out a deal with the Koressians."

"Even if the deal smells like a skunk with a toothache?"

Diego asked.

"What is that? Oh, well, never mind. Yes. Even though. Koress has large deposits of several important minerals. Which is why the Resh want the deal, too."

"Sounds like the Koressians are holding all the cards in the bruha game."

"Would you talk Seressian, for cat's sake? But if you mean they are pretty much in control, I would say you are right."

"So what are you going to be doing the next few days?"

"Going to His Excellency's winter resort to continue negotiations. Gossip says that a real big-shot is going to be there, too."

"Interesting, Rreengrol. Do they really want to make a deal with the Seressins, or are they enticing them for some other purpose?" When there was no immediate response, Diego asked, "Can you give me some idea where that is from the capital?"

"I can do better than that, my friend Diego. I can send you a map."

"Thanks." He waited, and when it came, Diego noticed how vast the desert was between cities. "That is a lot of territory if someone wanted to do something to a delegation."

"Yes, I agree. I have to go. I'll get in touch once I am back."

"Be careful, Rreengrol."

"I will. You do the same."

The face disappeared, and Diego stared at the screen for a while. The warning ding brought him back to his duties, and he sent in the necessary report. It wasn't too long before he was relieved. Sleep was hard in coming. It was like he had a great many pieces of a puzzle, but he couldn't figure out the way they needed to go together. He was missing something.

Chapter Fourteen

"Bress, how does one go about changing duty stations?"

"One doesn't, unless you count doing something stupid that irritates the slave leaders."

"Oh, no, I don't want to do that."

"Why would you want another duty? What you have is considered easy."

"Boring, Bress, boring. No, I was just wondering."

For the next several duty sessions, Diego looked up hydroponics, curious about how they worked. It also helped that it was near the cargo and escape shuttle bays. He studied the Koressians as well, wanting to know more about those desert warriors. There was little in the library about them, but there was a picture. He studied it carefully for some time. There was something about it that made the hair on the back of his neck stand up, something that wasn't quite right. After a while, he gave up and went to other topics. There was a great deal about the importance of Koress. Diego studied all the information about natural resources and placement of the planet in the galactic quadrant.

Finally, the cat face showed up early on the fourth duty cycle since he last talked to Rreengrol. Diego breathed a sigh of relief until he saw the little cat angrily lash its tail and growl.

"What's wrong, Rreengrol?" Diego asked.

"The commanders are signing an alliance with Koress."

Diego felt his stomach drop. "How soon?"

"The high commander can be here in three days."

"Where is it going to be held? At that palace you were at?"

"Yes. Away from crowds and other city distractions."

"Does this place have a landing field?"

"For smaller shuttles, yes, but for larger craft, no."

"In other words—"

"There would be no quick and large force back-up in case something went wrong."

"Did you tell Commander Hreeshan your concerns?" Diego asked hopefully.

The face grimaced. "Yes, I finally got my master's ear, and at first, I thought he was going to listen to me. But then he told me that all precautions were being taken. I was to let him and his fellow commanders command."

"In other words, that is why we are squires, and they are commanders. Or rather you are."

"Exactly. I'm pretty sure it's going to be three days."

"Keep me up on what's going on."

As it was, it ended up being Gorlis who gave Diego particulars. The thin Seressin came to visit with him right before his sleep cycle. Everyone gave them wide berth. Diego knew it wasn't going to be good. "Did your investigations reveal anything?" he asked hopefully.

"No, but it would have been no matter. Part of the treaty making Koress part of the Seressin Empire is that you will be turned over to the Koressian leaders."

"What? I thought—"

"Commander Ziron fought hard to take that out of the negotiations, but Koress was adamant, and the supreme commander wanted the alliance completed as soon as possible. "

"For the fuel ore, mithrin deposits, and melirin extracts."

Gorlis sighed. "That pretty much sums it up. Ziron really did not want this, Diego, but the commander is not the only one working on this. The supreme commander overrode Commander Ziron's objections."

"When am I going down?"

"The day after the signing."

"How many days is that?"

"Three days. The signing will be the day after tomorrow."

"Rejas, may I confide something to you?" Diego asked.

"Of course, Quirlis," Gorlis replied.

That took Diego aback. Gorlis must have some idea of the Koressian's duplicity. "Do you believe me?"

"Yes, I do, Diego. But sometimes that is not enough."

"I know." Then he told the counsel his suspicions.

"How did you learn some of these things? This is since you came back aboard," Gorlis pointed out.

"I really can't tell you, sir."

"I understand, and to your credit, I, too, feel there is something not right."

Diego thanked Gorlis and headed to the sleeping room.

Again, sleep did not come easily, and when he finally did fall asleep, it was filled with strange dreams. It was the last one that had him leaping out of bed searching for a weapon. This time he had been in the desert, but it was near a small landing field. Several small ships and shuttles were lined up at one end, with a procession of vehicles nearby. An older but still powerful looking Seressin was standing near Ziron and his sub-commanders. Rreengrol was with his rejas, each squire standing behind his commander. *The older commander must be the high commander*, Diego thought. Another, even older Seressin leader walked up to the group and began a conversation. From the uniform, this one must be another high commander. Diego couldn't understand what they were saying, but the high commanders were in very good moods. Commander Ziron smiled, but his eyes showed a hint of unease.

Three Koressian guards walked up to the group and directed them toward the vehicles. In the distance, Diego saw several tall, light-colored buildings. He remembered from the map that it was several furlongs from the landing field to the palace. All of the Seressins and their squires walked toward the vehicles, tall and dignified. This time, the squires were not separated from their rejas. All entered vehicles, two commanders and their squires per vehicle. Perhaps the commanders had set their hosts straight on Seressin protocol. Regardless, the procession started forward across the gritty, sandy soil toward the buildings in the distance.

The group was about halfway to the palace on the desert road when everything came apart. Laser rockets began firing, blasting chunks of road everywhere. Several dozen desert warriors rode out from behind rocky outcroppings on strange but fast creatures. They surged toward the vehicles, firing long-bored weapons that resembled muskets from his homeland. What they fired was much deadlier than any musket. Incendiary blasts blew apart whatever they hit. The creatures the warriors rode were six-legged, but built something like the horses he had grown up with. Their hooves were as big around as dinner plates, their heads broad, with bared teeth that ended in points. The eyes were large and deep red. Diego did not doubt that these creatures ate more than grass. The first attackers were killed before they were more than two horse-lengths from the rocks, but more continued to pour from behind the rocks.

Injured mounts screamed as they writhed on the ground, but the warriors made no sounds, except to beat the butts of their rifles against something hard on their saddles. It was a clacking racket that reached deep into the skull, disorienting their victims. A flash erupted near one of the cars, and the following boom sent the vehicle over on its side. The commanders leaped from their vehicles, their weapons drawn, their squires right behind them. They fired, but they were up against too many on animals that were too fast and extremely aggressive. Although the Seressin contingent killed many of their attackers, soon, the desert warriors were swarming over the commanders, shooting at point blank range, or clubbing them with their rifle stocks.

Rreengrol shot several of the horses out from beneath their riders. Diego could hear him telling the other squires to do the same. Wors was standing near Ziron, shouting expletives at the enemy, using his bolas to knock several

Koressians from their mounts. But it was useless. Before the shuttles could come and help the rejas and squires, they had all been slaughtered. Even one of the shuttles was blown from the air, crashing in a ball of flame near the road.

Diego could smell the burned flesh, feel the heat of scorched metal. He could see Ziron and Rreengrol laying lifeless on the desert soil. The warriors took long knives and made sure that all of the Seressin and their companions were dead. They stripped the commanders of their badges of rank. Mounting their creatures, they dashed up and down the road until the other shuttles began screaming toward them. Then as quickly as they had appeared, they disappeared back into the rocky hills. It was like they were made of smoke, but Diego knew they weren't. They were real. He knew it in his gut, which was roiling with revulsion at the events in his dream.

The shuttles flew back and forth, searching, but could find nothing of the warriors except the dead and wounded who had been left behind. One of the creatures lay writhing on the sand, screaming a high-pitched squeal that hurt Diego's ears.

Suddenly, laser fire cut down the remaining four shuttles, which exploded into fiery, twisted pieces that blew upward and then rained down on top of the dead bodies. Koressian soldiers arrived shortly, searching the scene of carnage. Diego saw the foremost soldiers carrying the same kind of weapons as the mounted warriors. They made sure that all in the entourage were dead.

Diego woke up gasping for air, his body drenched in sweat. "Rreengrol, Commander," he cried out. This was not some nightmare, this was a foretelling. There were two days, two days to prevent this. But how could he do it when no one would listen to him?

"Diego?" a voice whispered. Something climbed up into his hammock with him, but it took a second to realize it was Bress. "You saw death. The death of the leaders."

"Yes," Diego said in a shaky voice.

"This is happening in two days?"

Diego had long since quit questioning the little otter-people's abilities. "Yes, unless we can figure out a way to stop it."

"How do we stop it?"

"I don't know right now. But I have to figure something out." He gazed into the glowing eyes. "We need anyone who will believe us."

Chapter Fifteen

"My family believes you and will help."

"Thanks, Bress, but we need more! Do you think Lurin would listen?"

Bress rubbed his chin. "Don't know. Does he like you?"

"I can't say, but we have to try anyone."

"How do we get down to Koress?"

"The escape shuttles," Diego stated.

"Can you fly one?"

That took Diego aback. That was why he felt Lurin was a key to their success. "I have done some tutorials."

Bress chattered his laughter. "On the computer? We need more than that, my friend. We need pilots. I will go see my family right now. They will know who else to ask and who might know how to fly."

"Thanks, Bress. And we will need to go down the night before this treaty signing."

"Yes, I know. Tomorrow night." The little creature loped down the corridor.

Diego knew Bress would be the key to getting help in saving the commanders. It would help him in getting the backing of the master, Lurin. He lay back down and tried to sleep, but the dream kept replaying itself over and over in his mind. Finally, Diego pulled on his coveralls and slipped on his boots. He snuck out of the sleeping room and headed down into the deeper levels where he worked and where Lurin's quarters were. The slave master should be awake by now.

Bress waited near the master's portal for him, along with a large group of the little creature's family. Diego was disappointed there wasn't more support, but understood that even though he wanted it instantaneously, Bress needed time.

"Many more would like to help, but there is no room for all to come," Bress told him.

He waited at the portal that led down to Lurin's quarters, hoping to hear some indication that the master was awake. The dull red light was all he could make out, along with a wheezing/hissing noise that Diego assumed was Lurin sleeping. Regardless, he started down the ladder, slowly, listening to see if Lurin woke up.

"You should wait. The rejas does not like anyone coming to his den," Bress told him.

Diego paused on the fifth rung, undecided. Lurin had made it clear that he was not to be bothered in his own quarters, but this was important, a matter of life or death. "We don't have time!" he replied to Bress.

"What if he refuses to believe you...us?"

Diego didn't want to believe the Seressin might turn them down, or worse, turn them in, but that was a possibility. Still, they had to have the help of one of the masters. Lurin was the obvious choice.

Diego climbed down a few more feet. "Lurin," he called in a loud whisper. "Lurin!" A little louder, "Lurin! I need your help. Rejas Lurin?"

There was a growl from below, and then a shouted, "This had better be important!"

"It is, Rejas Lurin. I promise!" Diego shouted back. He could hear the rejas slowly climbing up the ladder. Finally, Lurin's reptilian face materialized from the dimness below. Diego scrambled back up the ladder and sat away from the edge of the hatchway.

Lurin's head showed. "What is so important that you have to come and wake me?" he demanded.

"I'm sorry, Rejas, but the commanders on the surface are in great danger. They will be massacred the day after tomorrow during the signing of the treaty between your people and the Koressians."

To his credit, Lurin didn't immediately respond. After a pause, he asked, "What intelligence have you received to come to this conclusion? Or is this the delusion of one condemned to Koressian justice?"

"Justice?" Diego asked, outraged. Then he felt Bress's hand on his arm, and he calmed. "No, sir. I don't care that much what they do to me. They have already tried to kill me. But they are planning on killing all the commanders, even the high commanders, and their squires."

"Again, what brings you to this conclusion?" Lurin was now sitting on the deck in front of them. That was something Diego had never seen any of the other Seressins do.

Diego took a deep breath and told Lurin his dream. Again, Diego was hopeful when the master didn't say anything immediately. "Sir, I believe this is a true dreaming of what is to come."

"Ziron picked you because of *his* dreams. Many thought he was crazy. Some think he is crazy to believe in such things, but it has brought him to the point where he is today, and in such a short time. I wonder if he also picked you because he felt you would dream truly as well." Lurin gave a huffing sigh and shook his head. He scowled. "I cannot go by such things," he said loudly, glaring at Diego. He hissed, giving further indication of his displeasure. His anger erupted. "This is silly hatchling chatter. Go away and let me get back to my sleep." He grabbed Diego's arm and shook him hard enough to make his shoulder creak. "You and anyone listening to your chatter are idiots! I will put you on clean-up detail for this craziness, and especially for waking me up. Next shift, you will report to shuttle bay six, and you will do waste detail," Lurin ordered.

Waste detail! That entailed cleaning out the bathroom facilities of the shuttles, as well as working the recycling plant for waste generated on the entire ship. It almost made him gag to think about cleaning the excrement of so many beings. Although Diego was angry and disappointed, he remembered to look properly chastened before Lurin handed out something even worse. He hung his head. "Yes, sir. I...I am sorry."

"The rest of you will be doing the same thing next shift. Get out of here now before I make it permanent!" Lurin shouted. "How many of you are in on this?"

Bress stammered, "About two hundred, Rejas."

"You are all sewer scum. I'm putting all of you on waste detail. And don't be late, or it will be permanent duty."

Bress and his family scattered. Diego followed more sedately behind them. How could he have so badly miscalculated? How could he have thought any of the masters would be willing to believe him and his dream? What were they going to do now? Or rather he. He had gotten Bress and his family members into this.

Diego wasn't aware of a tugging on his sleeve until it became violent enough to jerk him off his feet. It was Bress. "I'm sorry, Bress. I didn't mean to get all of you in—"

Bress was hissing his pleasure. "Don't understand," he began in a soft whisper.

Diego leaned down to hear his friend.

"Lurin is on our side."

"He has a strange way of showing it," Diego responded.

Bress hushed him. "It was hard to feel his thoughts. I guess even masters have to worry about being heard, but I think he sent us down there to be ready."

Diego was speechless for a moment. Shuttle-bay six! That was a real shuttle, not one of the escape pods.

The otter-man wiggled his short whiskers and gazed meaningfully into Diego's eyes. "Question is, will we be ready when we are down there?"

Diego knew he was talking about a pilot. He sat down on the deck so he could talk more easily with his friend. His back was sore from bending over. "Isn't there always someone down there with the shuttles? A student pilot, if not a master?"

Bress shrugged. "You're the one who's been studying

shuttle piloting."

Several other members of his family began milling around. They stroked each other as though consoling one another. Diego knew it was diversionary in case some rejas came along; or worse, someone who liked to curry favor by telling on uncooperative slaves.

"I think that is what they do. We'll find out tomorrow night."

"And if they don't?"

"I'll pilot myself." Diego stood. "I have a tutoring session to attend. Need to learn more mechanics for my job tomorrow," he said in disgust, loud enough for someone who might be listening.

"Don't forget to add sleep to your list of things to do," Bress reminded him with a knowing wiggle of his ears. He and his kin pattered down the hallway.

If Lurin was on their side, would he do more than assign them a job near the shuttles, Diego wondered? But what else might he be able to do? He shook off the negative thoughts and headed to a free computer station. He tapped in a public access code, not wanting to make it easy for a rejas to figure out who was looking up shuttle piloting. Memorizing the controls and what each did was easy. It was the real piloting that was going to be an issue. You couldn't march into a shuttlecraft and start it up. You had to have clearance codes, for one thing. Diego had only driven a carriage in his short life. He had been taught a little about riding and controlling a hoverboard here on the ship, but that was a far cry from a shuttle.

He still continued, learning how a shuttle was prepared

for take-off, how it was taken out of the bay, some of the control functions. Navigation was a lot trickier, and his eyes were burning before he finally gave up.

When he went into the dining hall, word had already spread about his and Bress's new assignment. Laughter followed him throughout the hall, and taunts were flung with every bite. Diego did his best to ignore them. Bress sat next to him with several of his brothers and sisters. They whined and did their best to look pitiful. When he didn't respond to the teasing, their tormenters left them alone.

"We'll be working a full duty shift before it is time to…." Bress didn't need to finish that sentence. "You need to sleep before we have to report. You look like a frinseckian clam in a dry up."

"Thanks, I think," Diego responded. He tossed his half-eaten lunch into the recycler and left. Bress and the others followed him.

His friend scampered in front of Diego and stopped. "Get rest. You may be the one to fly the shuttle," Bress admonished. The dark eyes showed confidence and trust.

Diego hoped he could live up to that trust. He nodded and headed up to his sleeping quarters. Jesk was in the hammock, so Diego found an empty bunk. Again sleep was hard in coming—mainly, he thought, because he was afraid of another nightmare. However, he finally did fall asleep, and there were no dreams. He woke to someone shaking him awake. It was Jesk, grinning broadly.

"Wouldn't want you to be late to your first shift at your new job," he smirked.

Diego wanted to shove Jesk's teeth down his throat, but

instead, he decided to irritate him. "Thanks, Jesk. I wouldn't want to be late, either. I think the job will prove interesting." He clapped Jesk on the shoulder and grinned back at him, all the while thinking what an understatement he had made.

He jumped down from the bunk, washed up quickly, and headed toward the transport that would take him down to the shuttle bay. Bress and his kin caught up with him. There were several other beings with them. The crowd was definitely larger than it had been before. Bress had come through. Diego figured there had to be more than two hundred there.

"Great job, Bress," he whispered to his friend. "You can trust these others?"

Bress tapped the side of his head and wiggled his whiskers. Diego got the message.

It took several trips on the transport to get them all down into the bay. The slave master in charge, a small Seressin, gaped at them for a minute and then growled, "What are all of you doing down here? Sightseeing?"

"No, Rejas. Lurin sent us down here for waste detail," Diego answered.

There was another moment of silence, then he laughed. "What in the world did you do to all get sent down here?"

"Mischief, sir," Diego answered promptly. He certainly didn't want to go into his dream.

"Lurin needs to tighten the chains if this many of you are getting into trouble at once." He shook his head. "All right. Lockers with your gear are in there." He pointed toward an enclosure on the far side of the bay. "Don't have enough gear for all of you. You Turengen will clean pipes and disposal vents. Make sure you watch the schedule. Wouldn't want any of you getting sucked out into space." He studied Diego and his bigger companions. "You put on the larger suits and empty the waste units on each shuttle."

Diego nodded his acquiescence and headed toward the enclosure to get his gear. The suits were bulky and hot, but they would also keep the worst of the waste off his body. The master was waiting for them when they were in their suits.

"Come with me. The Turengen have done this before. They know what they are doing, but I doubt you do."

Diego had studied the tutorials on this one, too, but wanted the rejas to show him anyway. If nothing else, it would waste some time on their shift. He mentally grimaced at his own pun. They watched the master show the method for detaching the canisters and wheeling them to the main disposal and recycling units. It looked simple and safe enough. Diego was wondering why they had to wear the awkward suits.

As though the rejas could read their thoughts, he stated, "Keep the suits on at all times working with these canisters. They not only contain waste, but also the material that begins the breakdown process. If any of that would get on you, it would cause serious damage, possibly death, to you. The stuff coating the insides of those canisters will breakdown any kind of biological substance."

"But how can you recycle any of this if that kind of stuff is in these containers?" Diego asked.

The Seressin shrugged. "I don't know for sure. I think it's because it breaks down quickly. Don't worry about it. If you do this right, you won't have any problems."

"Yes, Rejas," Diego and the others answered dutifully.

They set about their task, two of them hauling each

canister over to the recycling unit. They sealed the waste container to the intake portal and pushed the button that would suck the waste into the recycling unit. It took strength, but little thought. It wasn't long before Diego was feeling unused muscles protesting.

"When do we take the shuttle?" Renth, his partner, leaned over and asked. Renth reminded him of a rock lizard, except he was much bigger. He was quite strong, too. Despite being a head shorter than Diego, Renth could almost lift the containers by himself.

Diego glanced around, making sure there was no one listening nearby. "Near the end of the shift, a short while before the next group comes in."

"Heard there wasn't going to be another waste detail until second shift tomorrow," Renth hissed back.

"How do you know?"

"I overheard the master telling someone on the communicator when we were changing into our gear. He said he had so many slaves working the detail that there wouldn't be anything for the next shift to do." Renth chuckled. "He must have thought he had won the interplanetary lottery when Bress's family showed up."

Diego had no idea what Renth meant by a lottery, but he didn't want to ask. "That works in our favor, but I still want to be ready to take one before anyone new comes around."

Renth nodded. "Makes sense."

They worked in silence until near the end of their work period. Diego motioned toward the nearest shuttle. He saw Bress and several of his family meandering toward him. They were covered in dust and goop, and he smelled them long before they came within talking distance. Diego waved his hand in front of his nose.

"Can't clean off, or we will look suspicious," Bress's sister, Jeng, said.

"How come?" Diego and Renth said at the same time.

"We are going into the shuttle to clean lines. You do not go wash and then get into smelly waste again." Jeng wiggled her whiskers, and a glop of something unidentifiable dropped off and splattered on the deck.

Diego groaned. To be cooped up in a shuttle with all those nasty smelling creatures wasn't his idea of fun. However, he understood their logic and couldn't come up with anything better. He nodded and watched the group march up the shuttle ramp.

"Let's get this canister filled, and then we can join our stinky friends," he told Renth.

"Maybe we'll scare the Koressians with the smell."

Diego couldn't help it. He laughed.

Chapter Sixteen

By the time they finished that canister, they saw others heading for the shuttle. It was a good-sized ship, but Diego was wondering if they would all have room to fit inside. He squeezed through the hatch and made his way to the flight deck. Diego recognized the instruments, but almost froze at the complexity of them. He took a deep breath to calm himself, something made much more difficult by the smell of Bress and his kin.

"Can you figure this out?" Bress asked him. The Turengen was right by his elbow. Diego had to work to keep from gagging.

"I hope so."

Bress backed away a step. "I hope so, too. I cannot imagine what will happen if the Koressians do this thing they have planned."

Diego thought about that a moment. "I wonder if they realize what will happen, either."

"What do you mean?"

"What do you think the supreme commander will do to them?"

"Oh," Bress said in a tiny voice. "They would come after them with their warships."

"It makes me wonder what they are thinking about. Why are they doing this?"

Bress was quiet for a moment. "Do you think they are allied with the Resh?"

"And the Resh are wanting to start a war with the Seressin? I think you're right, Bress."

"Which means we are not even safe on this ship."

"Which means we...." Diego began to say they might not succeed even if they did save their commanders, but he chose not to. He had to believe that they could do this. "Let me study these controls for a moment. Then I need to figure out how we are going to get clearance to get out of here."

"Leave that to me," a gravelly voice barked from the doorway to the control deck. It was Lurin.

Diego was never so glad to see someone in his life. "Rejas! I....I...."

"I didn't figure you had thought this all the way through," Lurin grumbled.

"I wasn't sure of everything, Rejas," stuttered Diego. "I just knew we had to get down there, and I didn't know—"

"Squire," Lurin began. "I was not sure of your story at first. Actually, I was not sure of you, but I see that you are serious and believe what you have seen." He gave a hissing breath between his teeth. "I have contacted your counsel, and there is much to be suspicious of with the Koress."

"Indeed there is, and much to be suspicious of in your

behavior, Slave Master Lurin," said Gorlis.

Whereas Diego had been almost ecstatic when Lurin showed up, now he felt hopelessness settle in. Gorlis would stop them.

"I believe the squire," Lurin declared.

"So do I," Gorlis replied.

"You do?" Diego stammered. "

"Yes, I do, but we can't go barging down there without some kind of plan. Something that won't look like an… invasion."

"You're turning me in," Diego said in a rush. "You're just doing it early. You won't be able to wait."

"That sounds as lame as High Commander Crelish's grandfather," Lurin said with a snort.

"Then what?" Diego was feeling desperate. So close.

"Then we try it, because we need to do something, and I can't think of anything better," Gorlis added.

"We are going down…now?"

"If your dream is true, we need to go soon. We need to be there before the ambush. It is only a few hours before dawn where the Seressin delegation is being housed." Gorlis rubbed the scales that lined his jawbone. "Is this your army?" he asked, looking around at the crowd of Turengen in the shuttle. It was almost shoulder to shoulder. The back section of the shuttle was probably as crowded.

Bress bristled. "We are not big, but we are strong and are fierce fighters," he declared.

"I don't doubt it. But again, we need a plan, or at least some idea of how to do this," Gorlis responded.

"Diego," Bress began.

"Yes?"

"You said they had mounts of some kind? Animals they were riding?"

"Yes, something like the horses of my home world."

"We are good at baiting and harassing large animals like that. Set down close enough to let us get near the attackers. Their animals will not know we are there until it is too late," Bress explained. "And you are piloting?"

"With my help," Lurin said.

"And mine," another voice declared from the hatch.

Diego spun around and stared at the newcomer, a young Seressin who could have been a squire. This one was someone he had never seen before. "Who are you?"

"Prengi. One of Bress's cousins is my servant. He must have known that I would want to be part of this adventure. He had no trouble recruiting me."

"No adventure. We are trying to save commanders and high commanders," Diego said. "You can pilot a shuttle?"

"My training is for pilot. So yes, I can."

"Your training…."

Prengi frowned briefly before he gave a short bark of hissing laughter. "I have at least done practice runs. Have you?" he asked Diego.

He had to shake his head. "No, I have only done the simulation tutorial."

Prengi smiled. "That's a start. You can be my assistant. We will go in fast and skim low. Hopefully when we are low enough, they might won't be able to get a good fix on us."

"And if they challenge us?" Diego asked.

"Then I will be standing by with my story about bringing

the miscreant down," Gorlis added.

"Let's go, then!" Lurin declared. "We'll see if we can keep this part of the galaxy from blowing up in our faces."

Diego looked at him in surprise. That was the most animated he had seen the lower level slave master since his demotion.

"Come on." Prengi grabbed Diego's arm and shoved him toward the pilot's deck. They had to squeeze by the crowd of Turengen.

"Whoa! Wait a minute. Don't we need to get some weapons?"

Lurin took a tiny device from his jacket, which Diego recognized as a Seressin type of key. He pointed the key toward the deck and activated it. It hummed, and then four seams appeared. Bress helped him lift the top, and a veritable arsenal appeared beneath their feet. They were mostly hand held laser weapons, like the rifles of his homeland, but they were still effective.

"Are these good enough, Squire?" Lurin asked.

"They are!"

"We still need to rely on stealth and surprise," Gorlis added. "We cannot let it be said that we went down and started a fight."

"True. I guess we need to get there early enough so that we arrive before the so-called marauders," Diego agreed.

"What are we waiting for?" Bress asked.

"We take the weapons, but do not use them unless someone shoots at us," Lurin ordered.

"I hope they have bad aim," Diego quipped.

"Let's hope they don't even know we're there," Lurin

returned.

Prengi interrupted. "Which is why I think we need to leave now. It would be better if we could go in undetected."

"I think that is too much to ask the guardians of the star lanes," Lurin retorted. "But let's go."

Prengi went through the pre-flight routine at what Diego thought was a snail's pace, but was actually top time. The ship whined as it powered up. A reedy voice came through the speaker.

Gorlis didn't wait, he grabbed the comm-link. "We are taking the former squire planet-side to hand over to the Koressians. As part of the settlement."

"That was supposed to be after the signing," the Seressin on communications responded.

"I am grand counsel on this ship, and was ordered by the high commander to bring the miscreant down now," Gorlis answered tersely.

There was a pause. Diego knew he was holding his breath. By the silence, he judged the others were as well.

"Hmph. Continue."

Prengi engaged the repulsers, and the shuttle lifted easily, if not a little wobbly, from the deck. The shuttle doors opened, and they maneuvered into the shuttle lock. The door behind them thunked closed. There was a slight difference in air pressure and the change in the airlock indicators to show something was happening. Within a short time, the outer lock opened, and Prengi eased out into open space. "Here we go," he intoned. "Be ready to talk to surface control."

There was little for Diego to do. Prengi was pretty good for an apprentice pilot. Koress lay before them approximately a hundred-thousand leagues away. Diego studied the instruments in front of them, including the computer printout that indicated other ships farther out. He pointed them out.

"The three closest identify as Seressin starships. Probably belonging to the high commanders. There are several other ships near the limit of the computer's range. Pretty far out. I can't identify them."

"Resh?" Prengi inquired.

"If so, they are bold. I will convey this information to the command crew. They probably already know about them." Diego tapped in a coded message to the mother ship before concentrating on their approach to Koress.

They swung toward the planet below in a wide elliptical path that would take them into a low orbit on the other side of the planet. Diego was little more than a warm body in the co-pilot's seat, but he paid close attention to everything Prengi did. It wasn't long before they received a call from Koress.

"You are unauthorized to enter planetary airspace," the voice droned.

Chapter Seventeen

Lurin took over. "This is sub-commander Lurin. I have been authorized by Commander Ziron to bring the Squire Diego to your authorities."

"That was to have been after the signing. You are unauthorized."

"That was before High Command ordered the human brought down immediately. A show of faith, I suppose," Gorlis interjected. "I am ship's council, and was ordered to come as well."

There was silence, and Diego hoped the Koressians were not trying to get a hold of the high commander. Prengi continued arrowing down to the surface as though there were no issues.

"The high commander has verified," the voice ground out. It sounded a little disappointed. "Land at the following coordinates and remain in your ship until ordered to disembark." There was a distinctive click of terminated transmission.

Diego was sure his expression mirrored Gorlis and Lurin's. The high commander went along with them? Did he suspect something?

"Well, that is an interesting development," Gorlis spoke for all of them.

"Of course, we won't be able to do anything sitting on the edge of a space port, even in the middle of the night," Lurin pointed out.

"Give me a few minutes, and I think I can come up with something." Prengi pondered for a short time, tapped a string of symbols on the computer, and then worked some of the switches. Alarms began howling, and the shuttle shuddered and then tilted crazily one way and the other.

Diego grabbed onto the arm rest as his shoulder slammed against the side of the cockpit. "What?"

"Hang on. System malfunction. We're going down in the desert," Prengi barked above the noise.

"Emergency! Emergency!" Lurin shouted into the comm-link. "Guidance malfunction! Major shuttle systems failure." Then he shut off the link. "I hope you can land this thing now that you messed up everything."

"Of course, Rejas," Prengi retorted. His reptilian face was split with a wide grin. "I'll set it all right when we are closer to the atmospheric envelope."

The craft gyrated toward Koress. As the shuttle bounced on the upper atmosphere, Prengi worked the controls, then typed commands into the computer. Rockets fired, and they sped up. Diego felt his body flattening against the seat, and it was hard to breathe. He knew what was going on; he had practiced high gravity maneuvering. This was much worse than he had experienced, though. The shuttle rocked from one side to the other, and shuddered like it was going to fall apart.

"Hang on to something if you can't fit into a harness!" Prengi called out.

"Do you have to bounce us around so much?" Bress moaned. "How are we going to fight if you scramble us?"

Diego threw him on his lap and re-adjusted and snapped the harness back on.

"They will blast us out of the sky if they think we've been faking. I'll try to make our landing as easy as possible, but I have to make it look good going down."

"I have had a bit of experience with transports, Quirlis," Lurin interjected. He was hanging on to Prengi's seat. "I can help you pull out when we get closer to the ground."

"Sit here, Rejas," Diego shouted over the noise of the sirens. He unbuckled the harness and was immediately thrown to the floor on top of Bress. He rolled over as the little otter-man screeched his discomfort. "Sorry, Bress." It was easier to lay on the floor than to try to get up.

Bress crawled up on his chest and patted his cheek. "I know you didn't mean to squash me, but I will stay up on top, if you don't mind."

Diego couldn't help it; he grinned even as he grabbed the bottom of the seat he had vacated to keep from sliding across the deck.

The shuttle bucked and rolled all the way down. Diego wasn't aware how near they were to the ground, but they had to be getting close. Finally, Prengi manipulated more switches, and the front retros fired, slowing the craft down.

Diego slid forward between Lurin and Prengi. Someone else slammed into his body from behind him. There were groans and a few curses.

"Make sure we're in one piece so we can take out those Fridian slime worms," someone shouted from the back of the shuttle.

"We will be," Prengi called back. "I hope," he added in a much lower voice.

"We will," Diego declared. "We have to."

The words were barely out of his mouth before they hit the sand, bouncing up into the air once and sliding forever before the ship came to a stop. Metal screeched and the console spit sparks, but a flame retardant spray kept it from bursting into flames. Lurin struggled with his harness, but finally got it loose. He rolled out of his seat, not caring where he stepped.

Diego jerked out of the way, but not before feeling the large saurian's boot against his thigh. The front ports were covered with something, and the emergency lights were slow in coming on.

"Let's get the weapons and get out of here before we have visitors," Lurin barked.

"Prengi," Diego called, pulling himself off the deck. "Prengi!" The Seressin had a gash on his head, presumably from hitting the instrument board. In the dim light, Diego made out Prengi slumped over in his chair. Diego feared the worst, but felt a slow pulse under the thick, rough skin of the Seressin pilot. It was normal for one who was dealing with trauma; a Seressin survival mechanism. As Lurin had, Diego had problems getting Prengi's harness undone. Bress jumped on the pilot's lap and helped. Soon Diego was pulling

Prengi to the back of the shuttle, where Lurin and Gorlis were manually cycling the hatch open.

"Let a couple of the Turengen take care of him," Lurin barked. "You hand out weapons."

Diego did as he was ordered. Lurin gave him the access code, and he quickly opened the locker. The smaller hand weapons went to the otter-men, while the large assault weapons were passed along to the Seressins and those of Diego's size. He handed out one of the last weapons in the cache and was surprised to see Jesk grabbing it from him. His astonishment must have shown on his face.

"I heard what might be happening down here. I may have no love for you, or for most of the masters, but if Lurin was coming down, I was, too."

"Good to have someone as strong as you down here," Diego said, and he realized he meant it. He climbed out of the storage bay with a laser rifle strapped to his back.

"You get the armor piercing grenades?" Lurin asked from the now open hatch.

"Are they in the locker?"

At the leader's nod, Diego jumped back down and noted several smaller bins recessed in the bay. They were filled with a variety of devices. He grinned up at Lurin and handed the bins up. The Turengen snatched as many as they could carry on their makeshift bandoliers. Bress looked like a porcupine.

He chittered his happiness. "Nice to make holes for beasts to step in."

Diego had to chuckle at the little warrior. He was small, but fierce. He didn't doubt that Bress's family would cause a great deal of damage.

Lurin handed Diego, Bress, and several others tiny communicators. "This will help us coordinate when the fighting begins."

Diego fit his in one ear and tested it.

"Let's go," Lurin said. "We don't have much time."

Diego wondered how far they were from the site of the ambush, and asked.

It was still dark, but there was a hint of light on the far horizon. Lurin pulled out a map and a small light. "We're here." He pointed at the map. "We need to be here in less than two hours." He pointed again. "A fast march will get us there with enough time to lay an ambush of our own. If we're lucky, that is. Grab a survival kit, and let's go!"

"What about Prengi?" Jesk asked.

"We'll leave him in a protected area with Gorlis. Someone can pick them up after this is all through," Lurin explained. "Now let's go."

They marched fast and hard. Diego sometimes slipped and fell in the sandy soil, but someone always pulled him up. With their webbed feet, the Turengen had no trouble, and Diego envied them. The sky lightened, but it was still gray when they reached the place of Diego's dream. He gasped at the exactness of the area. Never had he dreamed something that turned out to be this real.

"Where are they going to attack from?" Lurin asked.

"The commanders' entourage will come from there." Diego outlined where all the players would be. Bress didn't wait for the rest of his explanation. He chittered to his people, and they scattered, each of them taking a spot and digging. Diego couldn't believe how fast they worked. In less than two minutes, he couldn't see any evidence of them.

"Take the rocks, and make sure you won't be seen by the invaders. They will have to lay ambush, and I don't want them seeing us before we want them to," Lurin instructed. "And do not attack until they have made the first move."

"There will be an attack with artillery before the desert marauders assault the commanders," Diego told him.

"Where from?"

Diego closed his eyes and remembered. "From over there."

"Diego, you and Jesk check it out. We need to be able to neutralize it when the entourage gets here."

It was getting lighter. They scurried along the ground. Diego felt something trembling, and laid his hand on the ground. Something large was coming. The Rejas? He caught up to Jesk and whispered his ideas.

"Lurin and the Turengens will have to deal with things on the scene. We have to disable the big guns," Jesk hissed back.

They were now maneuvering within a rocky area. Formations rose around him. Perfect place for an ambush, but there wasn't room within these rocks. *Where would artillery be hidden?* Diego wondered. He leaned against one of the boulders. It didn't feel like a rock or anything natural. "Lurin, Jesk," Diego called into his communicator. "These formations are the battery. Camouflaged."

Lurin cursed. "Get up on one and see if you can spot some way to get into it. And tell me if you see the convoy yet."

Diego contacted Bress as he climbed up on one of the larger formations. They would need more of the explosive devices than the few that had been left to them by the otter-men. He saw a shadow flit over the sand even as Diego was whispering into the communicator. Continuing his search, he tried to see where the Koressians could be hiding such machines. A small leap took him to another boulder, this one larger. Diego hoped they hadn't heard his leap He kept looking for some kind of opening. Diego felt all around the rock, and finally discovered what might be a seam.

There was a humming sound from inside the rock. When he heard a soft chittering, he saw one of Bress's family sitting next to him.

"The enemy is inside the rock," Mors whispered.

"But we need to find an opening so we can throw in the bombs," Diego hissed back.

"Convoy is coming soon. We will see where they fire from in a short while."

Diego would have loved nothing better than to take these machines out right now.

"Have to let them make first move. They have to start it," Jesk reminded him.

Diego understood that, too, but it didn't make him feel any better. "How soon?"

Mors pointed, and Diego could see the dust from the column of vehicles.

"Where will riders come from?" the Turengen asked.

Diego pointed to a nearby outcropping of rocks. "It was so quick." He figured those were real rocks, but he couldn't be sure.

"Didn't see anyone. Don't smell anyone." Mors lifted his nose and wiggled his whiskers. "No, there is some place for them to come from, too. Here, take these devices. My sisters and I will look for places where riders could hide."

"Thanks for believing me."

Before Mors had scrambled halfway down the fake rock, it trembled and shook. Diego slipped and almost fell off, but he grabbed a projection and hung on. Jesk watched from another boulder, and from the way he was hanging on, Diego could tell that the entire battery was gearing up for the assault. The seam he had found split open. Diego readied a laser grenade and waited. He had a moment's warning from Mors before an agonizingly bright light burst from the interior. Even with his hands in front of his eyes, Diego was dazzled and disoriented. He heard the sound of other laser artillery and pulled his grenade out, arming it with a flick of a finger.

Diego still couldn't see, except through a curtain of tears, but he threw the device in the direction of the opening. He let go of his hold on the boulder and made his body relax, unable to see where he was falling. It still hurt, and it took a moment to catch his breath.

"Report!" Lurin shouted in his ear.

Diego gave a terse synopsis of what he had done even as the ground shook beneath his feet.

"I think it's about to blow!" Jesk shouted. "Get away from there, Diego!"

The problem was, Diego didn't know which way was away. He tried to scrub the smarting and blindness from his eyes, feeling a touch of panic at that thought, too. Then he felt a small, clawed hand grab his arm and tug. There was no argument; he followed. It had to be Mors.

They went a small distance before Mors chittered,

"Down!"

Diego dove for the dirt, and the ground behind him catapulted skyward. He felt himself lifted up and thrown forward. Smoke and dust clogged his nose and mouth, and he choked, trying to draw in a decent breath. Diego kept one arm over his mouth even as he crawled forward. A soft furry hide stopped him.

"Mors!" he hacked out.

Chapter Eighteen

Diego swiped his face with his sleeve. Through the haze that covered his abused eyes, he could see Mors lying unconscious under his hand. A quick examination showed that the Turengen was still alive. Smoke billowed all around them, and it was hard to take a breath. The screams of the beasts behind him told Diego that Mors's kin were doing their job.

Scooping up Mors and slinging him over his shoulder, Diego turned back to the battle. He pulled his laser rifle from his harness, and cautiously made his way forward. The desert wind blew away some of the smoke, and Diego could see the members of the convoy fighting the attackers. However, it wasn't the one-sided fight it had been in his dream. Many of the horse-like beasts lay dead or dying, and almost as many of their riders were dead. Blood flowed across the grayish gravel, making it look like black pools had been dredged in the road.

Now that he could see well enough, Diego picked off the

desert warriors still fighting. Part of him was telling him that he was killing thinking beings. They had families, friends.... *Stop it*! He had killed cougars and wolves that attacked the herds. These were trying to kill his friends. Diego continued to aim and fire, keeping Rreengrol in his mind.

He remembered the air attack and listened for fighters. A distant hum alerted him. "Lurin! Air attack, sun high quadrant!"

"Good. The batteries are down, we can concentrate on the attack forces."

"Yes, sir!"

Diego continued firing on the enemy, trying not to pay attention to the screams of the dying. Again he felt the bile creeping up his throat, and swallowed a few times. He had to save his marix, his friends.

The ground continued to shake, and another battery exploded behind him. Diego fell to his knees, dropping Mors. The little creature squeaked and hissed, but rolled over and stared around him. Blood trickled from a cut behind his high-set ear. He stared over Diego's shoulder and chuckled with delight. "Rocks gone. Nice flat land to fight on! Now let's get the rest of enemy."

"Make sure there are no more fighters in the batteries. I'll pick off warriors attacking the convoy," Diego said.

Mors staggered as he headed back toward the area where the fake boulders had stood, but it wouldn't do any good to say anything. Diego realized he was still a little shaky, too. He found a place above the road and began shooting anything and anyone attacking the convoy.

"Has anyone been able to contact the commanders?" he

asked over the communicator.

"A few of the Turengens have been able to make contact."

"The rejas need to abandon their vehicles. I don't think we can hold off the air attack."

"You're probably right, although the high commander's ship is coming in for support," Lurin replied. "I will have Bress head them your way. We are still dealing with those desert warriors. There must be hundreds of them!"

"I'll be watching, sir!"

Diego shivered, but it wasn't because of cold. Sweat trickled down his back, dampening his tunic. Tension tightened his muscles. He had to relax so he could be ready to help the commanders.

The second car in the convoy opened, and two commanders and their squires dashed out, weapons ready. One of the squires was Rreengrol. Diego almost stood up to give a signal, but there were too many of the enemy warriors. He fired on those still mounted. Several concussion bombs exploded like mines at their feet. Diego scrambled partway down and in front of a damaged artillery bunker, where the rejas could see him. He signaled them.

The warriors could also spot him. Laser fire surrounded him. The heat of the rays was intense. It was miraculous that none hit him, but a stench of burning cloth told him that they didn't need to hit him to do damage. He felt the sting of pain from some of those near misses. Diego slid down the bunker to escape the laser fire.

The pings of metal against metal evidenced the use of percussion-type weapons. Diego could not wait for the commanders to get to him. It would be safer to fight among them. He zig-zagged across the coarse gravel. His defensive training kicked in; he crouched low to the ground. Diego was almost halfway to the convoy when a column of desert warriors galloped out from behind the bunkers. No wonder it had seemed in his dream that the enemy had been everywhere. There was a place of ambush on both sides of the route. Why hadn't he noticed that in his dream?

Three of the warriors peeled away from their group to confront him. Diego shot one with his laser blaster before it had finished changing direction. It went down screeching. He raked across the second's legs. It screamed as well, but didn't go down. Its rider slid off its back as it reeled back. The third did something Diego didn't think possible. It leaped straight up in the air, avoiding his fire, and came down not two feet in front of him. The pointed teeth snapped at him, and Diego dodged back. He pulled a blast grenade from his arms pouch and activated it.

That was when he slipped on gravel and fell back. The beast pranced forward, and this time one of the cloven hooves came down on Diego's arm. The grenade rolled from his nerveless fingers. It would go off in less than eight seconds. He raked the beast's belly with his pistol. It jerked back and screeched, even as Diego screamed at the pain in his arm. It felt like it had been torn off. Still he rolled away, and staggered to his feet. The rider came at him with his long, knife-tipped lance. His agony blinded him to everything but that sharp tip coming at him. He tried to bring up his laser pistol, but his good arm rose slowly. The lance raced toward his neck.

Then the warrior went down, his clothing smoldering from someone else's blaster. A cry caused him to turn to where he saw another rider coming at him. Time slid back to normal, and he fired. Even though dead, the warrior slammed into Diego, and both went down. Pain shot up his arm and through his body. He struggled to shove the dead Koressian away, and after an eternity, Diego finally succeeded. Rolling to his side, he pushed himself up on his knees. His head was swimming, the pain keeping pace with his heartbeat.

Screams and explosions assaulted his ears. He saw the members of the Seressin convoy fighting the remaining warriors. Only a few were still on horseback. Diego fired at one, missing, but it swerved into someone else's fire and went down. He heard the hum and rumble of aircraft and looked up. Several fighters were streaking overhead, followed by a larger space craft that was firing on them. That had to be the high-commander's assault fighter that Lurin had talked about. Though under fire, the enemy craft was still trying to get to them.

It was insane. Chaos in the air and on the ground. Before it disappeared over the horizon, a Koressian fighter blossomed in a bright flare of light. Diego staggered to his feet. His left arm hung useless; his tunic was in shreds. He still clutched his blaster and fired it anytime he saw one of the warriors moving.

Finally, it was quiet on the ground. Diego continued his slow journey to the convoy. He heard someone to his left and swung his pistol.

"Hold on, Squire!" called a familiar voice. It was Rreengrol. Blood trickled down the side of his friend's face. There was blood on his uniform, but he was grinning. "I was afraid the Koressians were up to something."

"They were," Diego replied. "Status?"

"Wors is dead, as are Frinx, Miterlee, and several of the high-commander's squires and commanders, but most of us are alive because of someone's foresight and the Turengens' ability with blaster grenades."

"Commander Ziron?"

"He is a bit beat up like the rest of us, but very much alive."

Rreengrol put his arm around Diego's torso and helped his friend the short distance to where the convoy was gathered between two of the ground vehicles.

Not that he disbelieved his friend, but Diego breathed a sigh of relief when he saw his commander. Ziron was helping another member of the convoy. Squires hovered around like bees, and Diego figured the injured Seressin was a high commander. Disengaging himself from Rreengrol, he staggered over near Ziron and stood at attention. Or tried to. His legs felt wobbly, and he shuddered from the throbbing in his arm. He waited for an eternity before Ziron glanced up and saw him there. There was no hint of surprise.

Now that he was there, Diego didn't know what to say, so he resorted to the beginning squire litany. "Rejas, what can I do to serve you?"

Ziron studied him for a moment. "What was supposed to happen here if you and your comrades hadn't come down?"

"Total annihilation, sir."

"A dream?"

"Yes, sir."

"You asked what you could do to serve me. I think you have already done that, Squire. Your actions have saved us."

Ziron gazed at the sky where the dog fight continued. "But we are still not out of the game pit."

Chapter Nineteen

The sun was gliding higher into the sky, and Diego was feeling the heat rise through the soles of his feet and beat down on his head. He could feel nothing in his left arm except pain. Sweat made his skin prickle. Diego struggled to remain standing.

"Watch for the shuttle, Diego. If you stand there in the shade, you can see the whole area—the sky."

Ziron steered his squire toward the shady side of the vehicle, making sure not to touch the injured arm. He sent another squire, someone from the medical team, after him. The med squire, a young Seressin, sprayed his shoulder and arm with something that numbed it almost instantly. He ran off to help others before Diego could ask his name.

Diego was vigilant, waiting for a shuttle. Would it come from Ziron's ship?

Rreengrol joined him. "You all right?"

"Yes," Diego lied.

"You look like something a pack of frell lizards chased

around and chewed up."

"Lord Ziron said we were still in danger."

"The Koressians don't want us to escape. I can't imagine why." Sarcasm dripped from the Grrlock's words.

With Rreengrol's help, Diego kept the remaining warriors at bay. The last few galloped away down the highway. Fighters continued to fly overhead. One dipped close to their position.

"Get down!" Rreengrol shouted, jerking Diego into to the gritty soil. Laser bolts tore up the ground near them.

Another ship dived down after it, and the squires could see that it was one of theirs. It fired on the Korressian fighter, both laser and laser-concussion bolts. They continued toward the horizon. Before entirely out of their view, a fireball lit the sky.

"Was that theirs or ours?"

"Didn't see any fancy maneuvering, so it had to be theirs." Rreengrol was proved right when the Seressin ship screamed back their way.

A larger craft approached from the sky above the desert. It was a shuttle, a little bigger than the one that had transported Diego and his "assault force." The markings showed that it was not from Lord Ziron's ship.

"High commander's ship. Come to get him and his commanders out," Rreengrol murmured.

"Why haven't there been more shuttles?"

"I don't know, unless there is more going on besides our upsetting of the party down here."

"When we were coming down, I heard something about ships on the outer fringes of the solar system. They weren't ours."

"Resh, I suppose. Guess they made a better deal than our people did."

"I was wondering why Koress would try to assassinate so many high officials unless it was to an enemy's benefit. I mean, how could they stand up to us without someone backing them up?"

"Exactly. Let's get down there to our rejas now that the ground force has been routed."

"You sure they aren't coming back?"

"Maybe, maybe not; but we won't have a chance to evacuate if we don't know the plan," Rreengrol replied.

They reached the commanders as the shuttle landed. The sub-commanders and squires took up positions away from the road, surrounding the shuttle. Diego was able to handle a pistol, and stood close to Rreengrol, ready for another attack. A dozen guardsmen swarmed out of the hatch, their rifles ready. The landing force's leader dashed to the commanders' position and conferred with them. Diego was pretty sure he knew what the conference was about. Ziron motioned the two squires over to him.

"We are evacuating. Unfortunately, there is no room for anyone under the rank of sub-commander. Even some of those are staying behind. They will be your commanders. There will be another shuttle as soon as possible."

"Is it permissible to ask why, Marix?" Rreengrol asked. "Why there are no more shuttles?"

"There is not much time, but yes, it is permissible. The Resh have an attack force inside the sixth planet, here to take out our ships when we had been destroyed. They went ahead and attacked, so most of our forces are occupied. Perhaps they thought we were already annihilated."

"It is as we thought, Lord Ziron," Rreengrol affirmed. "We will hold out."

Ziron grinned. "I know you will." His gaze centered on Diego. "You have acquitted yourself well. I chose rightly."

Diego felt his cheeks flush. "I never dreamed like this before, sir, but I knew it was a foretelling dream."

Ziron hissed between his front teeth, a sign that he was nervous. "And you acted on it."

"Lord Ziron, should we try to get to the shuttle that brought us here?"

Ziron shook his head. "No. You would be too exposed."

"Perhaps we could commandeer these bunkers," Diego mused aloud.

"Suggest that to the sub-commanders." A whistle broke off the conversation. "I must go. I would stay and fight, but I have been ordered."

"Vaya con Dios, my Lord," Diego said. He knew Ziron didn't believe in God or the Holy Mother, but it still felt right.

Ziron knew. "And the Lords of the Cosmos protect you, my squires."

They watched as Ziron entered the shuttle, and the hatch closed. As two Seressin fighters hovered overhead, the shuttle lifted. It quickly gained altitude, flanked by the smaller craft, and they all soon disappeared.

"Let's see what the commanders want."

The commanders were Lurin and another Seressin they didn't know. The unfamiliar leader deferred to Lurin. Diego wondered what he had done before living in the bowels of the spaceship. He couldn't have been too low ranking an official.

"This is Sub-Commander Morwon," Lurin said, pointing to the other Seressin. "We are going to reconnoiter these bunkers; see what's left in them. Let's do it before anyone from the city comes out and sees where we've gone."

He glanced at Diego and hissed deep in his throat. It was a sign of pleasure. Diego noticed the Turengen gathering. Their ranks were thinned out, but most of Bress's family had survived the attacks. Bress eased his way over to him.

"Sir? Lord Ziron said it would be too risky to return to our shuttle, but would we be able to go back at night?" Diego asked.

"If it's still there," Lurin replied. "They could have blown it sky high, especially since they now know that we are the ones who screwed up their plans."

"Too bad we can't swipe one of theirs," Bress grumbled.

Lurin was very quiet for a while. "You Turengens may be small in size, but not in brain matter. That is definitely an idea, especially since we're not that far from the space port."

"Wouldn't they expect that, too?" another squire queried.

"If they have any brains," Lurin growled. "But I suspect they are relying too much on the Resh, and that would make them careless. Bottom line is we can hope for rescue, but we need to come up with a plan to rescue ourselves."

"Dust from the city!" Wreen called out from the top of one of the bunker/boulders.

"Find a nice hole so we can get under cover," Lurin called out.

When the otter-man pointed one out, Diego couldn't help but think that the hole resembled a grave.

Chapter Twenty

Rreengrol must have had the same thought. "Were any of those convoy vehicles left intact?"

"What are you thinking?" Lurin asked.

"A few of us grab any that are usable and take off in different directions. One of us can check out the shuttle and see if Lord Gorlis and Prengi are still all right."

Lurin didn't waste more than a few seconds thinking. He began pointing at squires. "Hurry! You don't have much time."

Diego dashed off after Rreengrol and Jesk. The numbing spray was beginning to wear off, but he pushed the pain to the back of his mind. They tried the next to last vehicle, which appeared to be untouched by the fighting. Rreengrol jerked the dead Koressian driver from the seat, but he couldn't get it started.

"Let me try," Jesk growled, almost pushing Rreengrol to the passenger side. It wouldn't start for him.

"We should try another one," Diego suggested.

Jesk growled again. Tapping the side of his nose, he considered. "I think I know why we can't start this thing."

"Doesn't recognize the driver," Rreengrol said.

Jesk reached over and jerked the insect-like alien into his lap. He positioned the Koressian's hand on the joystick and the other hand on a button to the left. The machine whirred and then growled to life. It quit as soon as he took the stick himself. With a curse, he pulled out his knife and hacked off the alien's hands. "There is no other way," he muttered.

Diego tested his communicator. "Commander Lurin! Can you hear me?"

It crackled in his ear. "Yes. I hear you got one going. Great work!"

"Jesk figured it out. It only recognizes Koressians as drivers. Fingerprints or something like that. Do you want us to head back to the shuttle?"

"Affirmative. Don't try to contact Gorlis until you are close to the landing site."

"Yes, sir." Diego slid in the back of the vehicle as he told the others what Lurin had said. "Do you remember the way?" he asked Jesk.

"Of course." They sped away, spitting sand and gravel behind them.

Jesk steered a course between the destroyed bunkers and then out into the desert. It seemed like forever ago they had slogged their way across, but it had only been a few hours. Diego kept looking out the back for signs they were being followed. Aircraft were still speeding across the sky, but much higher. That didn't mean anything, Diego realized. The technology these people had was incredible to him. He had been told the Seressins could see a flea on the hindquarters of a dog from miles away. They also had the science to hide from others. It was entirely possible the Koress had the same technology, but he didn't think so. The Resh probably did, which might explain why Koress wanted to deal with them. Thing was....

Diego saw a fighter dropping from the sky. As it flew overhead, he could see it was a Koressian ship.

"We've been discovered. Hopefully they will think we're friends."

"Saw it," Jesk answered. "We're close, but with that thing overhead, we don't dare call Prengi."

They sped over a rise and saw their ship. It had cut a wide furrow into the sandy wash. That would make taking off difficult, but not impossible. There didn't seem to be any damage that would make the shuttle unspaceworthy. The group also saw an armored carrier and about four Koressian soldiers examining the shuttle.

"Ooops," Jesk said. "Stay down. Maybe they'll think we're some of their own." He slowed down as he approached. Two of the guardsmen watched, but no one fired. "I sure do hope no one's inside that carrier," he muttered as they came closer.

Just as they got within twenty feet, Jesk increased speed and spun the vehicle sideways, spraying the two guards with sand. He threw open the hatch, knocking down one of them. His pistol brought down the other one.

"Would've been nice for Jesk to warn us," Rreengrol muttered as he flowed out of the other side of the shuttle. He began firing as soon as he opened his door.

Diego slid out, his pistol ready. He wasn't nearly as

agile, but he was away from the vehicle by the time one of the soldiers blew out the windows. Tiny shards of glass peppered his back as he fired at the remaining Koressian. He switched the firing mode to wide range and sprayed the area. Rreengrol was already checking the carrier, while Jesk put in the access code for the shuttle. He opened the hatch and then jerked back as the muzzle of a laser rifle greeted him.

The voice that called out spoke Seressin.

"Gorlis?" Diego called.

The counsel poked his head out after the rifle. "Diego! Thank the cosmos! And the commanders?"

"Evacuated. Wasn't enough room for all of us," Rreengrol replied. "Prengi?"

"Still a little woozy, but I think he'll be all right once we are safe. Despite my recommendations, he checked over the shuttle's systems. Come in out of the sun."

"I'm glad he did," Diego said. "The shuttle is our escape from here."

"I'll stay at the door," Jesk told them.

"I am assuming the convoy was attacked?" Gorlis asked.

"It was as I dreamed."

"Dreamed?" Rreengrol asked, incredulous. "I thought someone must have intercepted some Koressian intelligence. No wonder you and Lord Ziron get along so well."

"Casualties?" Gorlis queried.

"Not too many, I think," Diego answered. "I need to contact Lord Lurin."

Gorlis gave a gurgling laugh. "So he's Lord Lurin now."

"He stayed behind with a sub-commander and the squires," Rreengrol snapped.

"Sorry. I knew he had been a commander until his retirement. I was not insulting his courage."

"I know, Rejas," Diego said. He had to call several times before he was able to raise anyone, and then it was the squire in charge of the airport reconnaissance team. "Need to contact Rejas Lurin."

"They're monitoring our communications. Get off!"

Diego cut the communications. How in the world were they supposed to coordinate their survival if they couldn't communicate? "We're on our own."

"I doubt Prengi can pilot right now."

"Can, too!" Prengi wobbled to his feet. Dried blood had crusted on one side of his face.

Diego had done several tutorials on first aid to augment what he had learned from Anaar during his squire training. He stared into Prengi's eyes. "Headache?"

"Small one."

"Then what has you weaving like a drunken vaquero?"

"Huh? No, I'm a little dizzy. Sitting on my butt too long."

Diego raised his eyebrows.

"You think this ship can fly?"

"I think so."

"Then let's go get as many of our people as we can and get out of here," Jesk called out from the hatch.

"Might be a problem if the Resh are causing havoc," Rreengrol commented.

"All the more reason to get out of here and back on the ships," Gorlis added.

"Come on, then," Diego said. "We have some of our fighters near the bunkers, and some testing the space port defenses."

Prengi made his way to the pilot's chair, a little surer of himself. Diego followed, sitting next to him. Prengi blinked at him. "And how are you supposed to help, winged like that?"

Diego grinned. "I still have a usable arm. Between the two of us maybe we'll make one good pilot. Besides, you are a fine one to talk with that lump on your thick head the size of a goose egg."

"A what? Never mind. Go ahead and do the pre-flight checklist. Jesk, lock the hatch."

Diego did as he was told, but before he had finished, Prengi fired up the engines, clearing out the clogged intakes. Then he engaged the lifters and righted the craft. Diego brought up the map, using the computer pointer to show Prengi the location of the bunkers.

"How many?"

"Most of the Turengen, about a dozen squires, Lurin, and a sub-commander."

"Do-able, considering how many we had in here on the way down. The force at the space port will have to take care of themselves. I think we'll be lucky if we can get out of here with those we are picking up."

"But we can't leave the rest of our force!" Jesk protested.

"They went to the space port to steal a ship, correct?" Prengi asked.

"Yes."

"Then that's what they'll have to do. We barely had room for our assault force — there is no way we'll be able to evacuate everyone left behind from the convoy."

Jesk scowled, but didn't say anything. There was nothing

else to be said.

"Strap in!" Prengi lifted slowly off the ground, testing the controls. When everything worked out, he eased the craft in the direction indicated by the computer. Then he jerked the control stick back, and the shuttle shot forward, slamming them into the backs of their seats. Prengi grunted, but handled the controls with a steady grip.

Diego gasped at how closely they hugged the ground.

"Harder for Korressian detection devices to track us."

"I hope no one holds up a laser blade," Diego quipped.

"Keep an eye on the forward monitor, and we won't have that problem."

"Yes, sir!"

Diego grinned as he kept his eyes on the surface before them. Prengi easily navigated the small hills and boulder strewn desert.

"There it is!" The damaged bunkers lay right ahead of them.

Prengi swung around several times before he decided on a landing place. "I hope they were paying attention. As soon as I land, Jesk, go find them and get them back here."

Jesk was cycling the hatch before the landing gear touched the ground. He jumped out and dashed around the nearest bunker.

"Commander Lurin!" Diego called. "Acknowledge, Rejas!"

"I said get off the radio! They are monitoring it."

"Sir, evacuate! Quadrant 611, evacuate."

There was a short silence. "Understood."

"Jesk."

"I heard."

Now it was a race against time. Could the Seressin force make it to the shuttle before Koressian fighters got to them?

"We're coming in!" Jesk called. "Hurry!"

Diego checked the computer. "A couple of fighters heading this way."

"Whose?"

"Can't tell," Diego answered.

"We'll have to assume it's theirs."

Chapter Twenty-One

Jesk clattered through the hatch. Seconds later, squires clambered aboard. Bress and his family leaped through the hatch last, pulling Lurin.

"Any more?" Diego called out.

Lurin shook his head. He was puffing like a bellows.

"Hang on, this is going to be fast and hard." Prengi engaged the lifters, but before the back struts were off the ground, he activated the thrusters, and they shot into the sky. Bodies slid along the deck. Curses sounded from the back of the shuttle, the loudest of which was Lurin's.

Diego crossed himself, hoping Prengi's maneuver would fool the fighters long enough to allow them to get out of the atmosphere.

"Hurry and find seats. I might have to take evasive action!"

As the shuttle broke free of the atmosphere, their passengers disentangled from each other and strapped themselves in wherever they could.

"All secure," Lurin called. "Located the ship?"

Diego studied the read-outs. "Yes, Rejas. They are quadrant 021. There are other ships. I think one is the high commander's ship. Others are probably Resh or Koressian."

"Resh, most likely," Lurin said. "I need your seat, Diego. I have to send the emergency recognition code, so we aren't blasted by our own people."

Diego unstrapped and slid out of the seat. Prengi still had his thrusters at max, and Diego fell in a heap on his bad shoulder. He bit back a groan. Several small hands grabbed and pulled him into a seat.

"Thanks, Bress."

The otter-man chirped, slid into the seat next to him, and buckled the straps. Diego closed his eyes and listened. The shuttle rolled, and he felt the pain of the straps digging into his shoulder. There was a bang. Lurin cursed, and Prengi banked the shuttle from one side to the other, evasive maneuvering. They were under attack.

"Resh," Bress hissed. He slid out from the harness and skittered to the back of the shuttle.

"What?" Diego asked.

"Laser canons," Jesk told him. "I should have thought of that myself." He unbuckled his harness and fell to the deck. With a growl, he crawled to join Bress.

That was out of Diego's limited knowledge, so he stayed put, praying the Virgin would intercede for them. Bress continued to amaze him with his abilities to figure out any weapon or situation. Did that come from his telepathic ability? The ship bucked, but Prengi held a steady course. Several other members of Bress's family scurried to the back of the ship to help. They were good at keeping their footing as the ship was buffeted around.

There was a flash on the portside monitor. The ship shuddered, the artificial gravity shut down, and the lights flickered. Lurin spat out a curse that Diego had not heard before as the Seressin commander helped Prengi control the little ship.

Jesk's fingers flew over the console. Diego felt the shuttle shudder every time Jesk fired. The monitor showed several enemy craft blossom and disappear. It also showed their mother ship. They were close now, but the fighting precluded trying to dock right now. Prengi shot underneath the huge craft and locked course between two weapon's modules. A rattling thump told Diego that the shuttle was magnetically attached. Jesk added his firepower to the mothership's.

Near misses shook the small craft and jolted Diego around. He bit his lip to keep from crying out. The hollow booming of the spaceship's defenses reassured him, but he sincerely wished this battle would end. It went on forever, then it got quiet. The noise of the massive engines within the larger ship broke the silence.

The shuttle jerked free of its mooring and shot forward along the belly of Ziron's ship. Lurin called out codes, and a bay opened ahead. Prengi eased them inside. The bay doors barely closed behind them before the ship shook from a blast outside. Several deep booms told of return fire.

"Out!" Lurin shouted.

They all unbuckled and scrambled toward the exit. Diego was in no hurry, despite Lurin's command. The idea of getting his shoulder jostled was not pleasant. Lurin was still waiting by the hatch when the rest had disembarked, and Diego was the only passenger still aboard.

"Like it so much you want to stay?" the Seressin growled.

Diego knew he wasn't angry. "No, sir. I'm just not as fast as the others."

Lurin nodded. "The shoulder hurts, and you're tired. I understand." He watched the young man climb down the few steps from the shuttle and closed the hatch. "You did well, Squire."

"Thank you, Rejas."

"Go to medical bay." Lurin grabbed his good arm to steady him. "The one on the squire's level."

Diego was startled. "Will Lord Ziron let me?"

Lurin guided the young man toward the bay exit. "Of course, unless he's stupid. If he doesn't want you back, which I highly doubt, then I will take you as my squire. Doubt I am going to be allowed to enjoy my retirement for a while."

"You mean that, sir? I mean, about taking me as squire?"

"I will account that stupid question to you being sleep-deprived. Of course, human! If not for you, we'd probably be floating out there with a bunch of debris instead of having a fighting chance of getting out of this alive!"

Diego tried to get his mind around what Lurin was telling him. He was so tired, though. Couldn't think.

"When was the last time you slept?" Lurin asked as they traveled up the ship's elevator.

Diego tried to calculate. It was that night before they took the shuttle. He hadn't been able to really sleep. Seressins valued their sleep. Their bodies thrived on it even more than his people. Maybe that was why most of the slaves were warm-blooded. He shook his head. "Couple of days, I think."

Lurin snorted. "No wonder you aren't functioning. Get some sleep under your belt as well as getting that shoulder looked at."

"But if we're in danger—"

"We'll be better off with well-rested warriors, Quirlis."

"Yes, sir."

"Don't sound so depressed. I suspect there will still be some action after you have rested."

The elevator door slid open. The corridor was the same one he had traveled down to go to his classes, his duty stations, and his meetings with Ziron. Several squires dashed out of an open door, almost colliding with them.

"Watch where you are going, you scaly oafs!" Lurin shouted.

They jumped back and gaped. Diego had trained with both of them.

"You're back!" Krenzk gasped. He grinned broadly.

Diego returned the smile. Krenzk had been one of the more pleasant squires. Diego enjoyed training with him. He nodded.

"Go on about your duties," Lurin growled. "Can't you see he's injured?"

"Yes, Rejas," the other squire answered.

Diego couldn't remember his name. He had begun training after Diego had been picked by Ziron.

The two squires trotted down the corridor and into the elevator Diego and Lurin had vacated. Lurin helped Diego into the medical bay.

The ship shuddered; the lighting flickered, but held.

"Take care of Ziron's squire. I need to get back to my post," Lurin told the med tech on duty.

Before Diego could say anything, Lurin was gone. The tech pointed to an exam table. He looked almost as worn as Diego felt.

"We'll take care of your wound first. Got it on Koress?"

"Yes."

"I heard it was a battle for the story crafters."

The ship shuddered again. "Doesn't sound like it's over yet," Diego muttered. He lay down at the instruction of the tech.

"Those treacherous slime bats have been trying, but don't worry; we've got some good fighters and firepower on this barge."

"I know," Diego replied. He sucked in his breath as the medical tech inspected his shoulder.

"Nasty looking. I'll put something on that will take away the pain. Then I'll do some tests."

As the medicine was rubbed onto his shoulder and arm, Diego felt himself drifting into sleep. He wanted to stay awake, but it was a losing battle. Before the first test, Diego was out. He didn't remember being escorted to a bed at all.

When lights over his head flickered red, then blue, then back to red again, he came out of his almost comatose condition and wondered what was going on. Diego was in the medical bay. Then he remembered — Lurin had brought him here to be tended to. He had fallen asleep. How long? What was happening? A distant siren blared.

"What's going on?" he called to a tech who was jumping nervously from one cabinet to another. Diego noticed that his shoulder no longer ached. They must have done a great job of fixing it, because there was very little discomfort. He didn't feel the deep exhaustion as before.

"Resh are attempting to board the ship!"

Resh? Diego hopped down from his bed. The med bay was almost deserted. He needed to get to his battle station. Then he stopped. His battle station would have been by his rejas's side.

"Marix Ziron said for you to report to the bridge when you woke up."

Diego didn't ask any more questions. He dashed through the hatch and up the corridor. The elevator wasn't working, so he sprinted toward the emergency access. His shoulder was stiff and made climbing the ladder difficult, but he still made it to the command level.

There was no guard at the entrance to the bridge. Diego pressed his hand on the ident-plate, hoping that his status was still in the computer. The door slid open, and he was hit with a chaotic cacophony of voices, machine noise, and sirens.

Lord Ziron was in his command chair, issuing commands and asking questions non-stop. Diego didn't dare interrupt, but did motion to another squire. "What is a squire's duty during this kind of event?" he asked in as soft a voice as he could.

Ziron heard him and swung around in his chair. "I want you to lead a contingent of squires and guards to the lower decks, where the first Resh will board. Lurin is in the armory and expecting you." He paused. "You have acquitted yourself well, despite the fact that you left a post." He grinned. "You have every right to rest, but it will take all of us to survive this."

Chapter Twenty-Two

"Yes, Marix. I am proud to serve, and together we will vanquish the enemy!" Diego repeated the oath of battle.

"I know." Zurin's eyes swept the command post. "All squires, anyone not manning a station up here, go with Quirlis Diego and repel the enemy!"

Diego felt new energy flowing through his body. He and the others ran down the corridors and scrambled into the working elevators. When the doors opened again, they pushed into the armory.

Lurin shoved various weapons and protective gear at them. Diego grabbed a gas canister and mask. He also shoved a blast pistol into his waistband. There were masks for most of the others, as well as a variety of arms. Diego snatched a pair of goggles that would let him see not only in the dark, but through the thickest smoke.

The group sprinted down to the shuttle bays, where it was most likely the Resh would try to breach the ship. Diego waited at the hatch.

"Let's go in!" someone shouted from the back of the group.

Terndal, another Seressin squire he had trained with for a short time, stood beside him waiting for instruction. Diego wondered how many other groups there were guarding possible entryways. "Are we the only ones down here?" he asked.

"Other than core crawlers?" Terndal asked.

Diego frowned. He had been a core crawler for a short time. "Yes."

"I think so."

"What if they come through somewhere else? We could be guarding the wrong place."

A tinny voice came over his earplug communicator. "Are you in position?"

"We are at shuttle bay 9," Diego answered. "Do you have information on where the Resh are?"

"Close to that location, Squire, but they are below."

Diego thought. What else could be down there? He turned to his group. Diego noticed some of Bress's family in the crowd. "Brenth," he called out. "Can you round up the workers? Get them to set up traps and deterrents in this part of the ship?"

"What are you thinking?" Terndal was looking at him like he was crazy.

"Access ports exist all over the ship, don't they? Places where workers can go out and work on the hull?"

"Well, yes."

"And we can't split up to guard each location."

"Right again. There's not enough of us."

"The Turengen are brave and effective fighters. They can hold this area and call us back if the Resh change their tactics," Diego replied.

Terndal looked dubious, but he nodded.

The lower level was more Spartan and cramped, meant mainly for engine maintenance. Diego smelled the odor of burned plastic and scorched metal as soon as the elevator door opened. The air seemed thinner. He sucked in a deep breath, but his lungs didn't seem satisfied.

"Hull breach!" he cried, jerking the breathing mask from his belt pouch. The others did the same. The small packet stretched over his nose and mouth, the membranes pulling in the minutest particles of oxygen.

The hiss of weapon fire came from not too far away. There was a haze of smoke drifting about knee high. "The Resh are coming aboard here. We have to protect the engines!" If the Resh got to the star engines they could cripple the ship and take care of the crew at their leisure. He gazed at his group. They were too few, and under-armed. "We have to spread out. We'll split up into twos. I'll send for more help." He made the quick communication to Lord Ziron and then motioned the others to different sections of this level.

The smell of destruction increased as he and Terndal continued down the corridor. Even with the rebreather, it was getting harder to pull enough oxygen into his lungs. A sound like croaking frogs wafted toward them. Resh! Diego motioned Terndal back to a side corridor while he plastered himself to the wall. They were just around the corner ahead of them. The clanking of weaponry against space armor was loud and harsh in his ears. So was his breathing, Diego thought.

He forced himself to calm down. The smoke was thicker; the scent of burning plastic was strong despite the efforts of the rebreather.

A squat, fat lizard rounded the corner. Several others followed, almost treading on the back of the claw-tipped, webbed feet in front of them.

Diego barely glanced at Terndal. It was the signal. He fired at the same moment Terndal did. Their blasts hit the lead Resh above the edge of his armor. The invader collapsed on the deck. Diego raked the other Resh, but this blast had less effect as the enemy jerked back around the corner. Both of them had hit their marks, though. The Resh soldiers weren't going to rest tonight feeling like they'd been to a party.

"Shock grenades," Terndal suggested.

Diego quickly considered the location of the ship's engines and shook his head. He contacted Lord Ziron with his information. "Nets," he ordered in a whisper. The small defensive grenades didn't explode to destroy their targets — they blew out steel hard netting that caught the enemy and immobilized him. He motioned for Terndal to follow him, and they crept forward. It was silent ahead. Diego didn't want them to end up like the dead creature before them. There was a slight intake of breath behind him, then Diego felt something beside his leg. It was Groosh, one of Bress's numerous cousins. The otter-man made motions, and Diego nodded.

Groosh slunk forward, creeping on his belly along the deck. He peered through the smoke around the corner and then signaled Diego. The other corridor was clear. Groosh pattered back to them. "Know of other way. Resh are waiting just beyond. Fry like frond fish at new year celebration."

"Where is this other way?" Diego asked.

Groosh continued back the way they had come. Diego tossed one of the net grenades behind them and was gratified to see it deploy perfectly. That would make it a more difficult for the Resh to follow them. He and Terndal followed Groosh. They reached the end of an even narrower corridor. Here they found a ladder similar to what Lurin had used to get to his quarters. Groosh pointed and then slithered down without a sound. Diego didn't hesitate. He used his boots to slide down the ladder and his gloves to keep from getting friction burns from the fast descent. Jumping aside for Terndal, Diego looked for their scout. Groosh was motioning from the shadows. If it continued this dark, that would be to their advantage. He adjusted his night vision goggles and joined the Turengen.

"How close are they to the engines?" he whispered.

"Not close. They are far enough for us to use these," Groosh replied, showing his belt of explosives.

Diego grinned. "Excellente! Let's see what we can do to make them regret coming aboard."

Groosh continued to lead them along the narrow corridor. They heard more of the croaking ahead and climbed up another access ladder to a maintenance bridge that ran across the corridor. It wasn't long before they were looking down on a Resh boarding party. There were a dozen of them, gathered around a hatch that appeared to have been blown.

Something shook the ship, and Diego almost lost his footing on the slender bridge. The Resh glanced at each other, and he surmised that this latest event was none of their doing. Their croaking sounded agitated. Diego wondered what had happened. However, now was not the time to worry about that—it was time to get their job done.

Diego motioned to Terndal, and they each pulled out several concussion grenades. As one, they activated them and tossed them below. The grenades skittered within a few feet of the invaders, who started screeching at the top of their lungs, or whatever they used to breathe. Diego and his group huddled at the far end of the bridge. The blast still knocked them flat and made their ears ring.

Diego attached a safety line to a hook at the end of the bridge and then crawled part way down the wall. He peered through the smoke to see what damage they had done.

The hatch was blown into space. Resh who were not tethered had also been blown out. What little air had been in the chamber was pulling at him as it whooshed toward the breach. Terndal jerked him back by his tether. They crawled into the next room and pushed the hatch shut.

"Few less Resh to give us grief," Terndal muttered as he pulled off his re-breather.

Diego checked the integrity of the air system and found that it was intact here. He gave a brief report to the command personnel and then considered his options. His communicator chimed.

"Squires, the Resh ship is damaged beyond their ability to use it against us anymore. However, there are still pockets of invaders in the lower levels. You must find and destroy!" Ziron's second in command told them.

"You heard him," Diego said. "Let's find them." He glanced at Groosh. If every group had a Turengen, it would save valuable time.

Groosh nodded. "Make sure one of my family is with warriors." He grinned and pointed to another part of the ship. "Several this way." Groosh pattered down the corridor, and the others followed close behind. The otter-man's belt was loaded with grenades and other weapons that bounced in rhythm to Groosh's gait. Diego pitied the Resh that cornered this little warrior.

They pelted down several corridors before Groosh stopped. "Where are they?" Diego whispered.

Groosh signaled quiet and stood statue still. Diego knew he was listening with his mind. After a few tense moments, he turned to them. "Several in the core engine room. Sabotage, most likely."

"Can we surprise them?"

Groosh shook his head. "They have guard listening." He paused in thought again, then his eyes lit up. "Yes. I am small enough."

"Small enough for what?" Terndal asked.

"Air revitalization vents. I can go in. Use gas grenade, and then signal you."

"Sounds like a good plan, Groosh. Where do you get into the vents?"

The Turengen sprinted down the corridor. "Here." He pointed upward.

Terndal was the tallest, so he reached up and undid the clips holding the grate over the vent. Diego lifted Groosh onto his shoulder. The otter-man jumped the short distance and was gone. Diego could not hear anything. If he ever rose high enough to have his own command, he would want Turengens to be a large part of the force.

"How is he going to signal us?"

Diego mentally groaned. He had forgotten to ask. "Knowing Groosh, he'll figure out a way. Let's head toward the engine room."

"But not too close. The Turengen said there was a guard."

"I know."

Before they reached the corridor leading to the engine room, a group of four more squires joined them. Diego signaled for complete silence. He also warned them to have their masks ready. After several minutes, he heard a muffled boom and then some tapping and banging noises.

A few seconds after that, Groosh's voice drifted out to them. "You take them, but be careful. Some got masks on before gas got to them."

"How does he do that?" Terndal muttered.

"A nearby vent," Diego said. "Let's get in there!"

As they started down the corridor, the hatch flew open, and the biggest Resh Diego had ever seen squeezed out, his two laser pistols firing. One of the squires cried out in pain. Diego threw himself to the deck and rolled back out of the line of fire. He tossed a gas grenade right under the alien's massive legs. A slight pop and the violet gas curled up around the Resh's body. The creature sneezed, roared an unintelligible oath, and continued its advance. Two more grenades bounced on the deck. By now Diego had his re-breather back on and was watching the Resh's advance, amazed the creature was still standing after the grenades and laser fire.

He had to be wearing something that offset the effects of their weapons. The Resh wasn't completely immune, though. Terndal fired his pistol again, and a croaking roar rattled the walls. Diego and the others fired until the huge warrior turned and hopped back into the engine room.

They followed, firing continuously into the still open door. They couldn't let the Resh barricade himself back in there. Apparently that occurred to the warrior, because he began to close the hatch. Diego directed fire toward the locking mechanism. It had little effect. The door continued to cycle closed. In desperation, Diego made a zig zag dash toward the hatch, pulling a concussion grenade from his pouch. The Resh warrior pointed his pistol at him, but Terndal and the others fired at the alien, providing cover for him. Diego pushed the activator button and shoved the grenade in the slit of space between the edge of the hatch and the frame. He threw himself backward onto the deck.

Someone grabbed his tunic and jerked him farther down the corridor. He felt a body on top of his. Then the grenade went off. The blast was like a live thing, a bull bearing down on him, roaring its anger as it came. The deck heaved and bucked. The air reeked of burned metal and something else — burned flesh. Diego tried to get up, but the body on top of him was heavy, and he didn't have strength enough to move it. He called to the person on him, but he couldn't hear anything.

Again, he tried to buck the body off his and finally succeeded. He called out to his team, but still, there was no sound other than a ringing in his ears, and Diego realized the blast had affected them. He couldn't hear anyone. A flash of panic was squelched down. He didn't have the luxury of going to pieces about his injuries.

Terndal lay unconscious beside him. Diego checked for signs of life, but couldn't find any. The squire had died trying to help him. The ringing in his ears grew louder. Diego looked around. Several other squires were picking themselves off the ground, shaking their heads and rubbing at their ears.

Chapter Twenty-Three

Diego painfully rose to his feet and signaled for the others to follow him. They crept toward the hatch, pistols ready. Tendrils of smoke drifted out of the engine room. Diego could barely hear the sound of a siren blaring from inside. Then a small, dark face peered around the hatchway.

"Groosh!"

The Turengen's voice sounded like a whisper at first. "All dead. From grenade or…." The otter-man stroked the barrel of his weapon.

Diego allowed himself a short smile. "Is that all of them?"

"Yes, now crews can come and fix damage."

Diego could hear almost normally now. There was a slight residual ringing. "Is it bad in there?"

Groosh shook his head. "Not too bad. If we can hold off Resh ships, it shouldn't take too long."

"Holding off the Resh; that's the trick. I'd better report to Commander Ziron." Diego tested his communicator and found it functional. He made the call. "Commander, the

Resh who came aboard have been killed. We have several casualties. The engine room crew needs to make repairs. There is a breach in the hull at V4461."

"Excellent! Report to the bridge, Squire."

"Yes, sir."

The trip took an interminably long time. Groosh accompanied him, casting his small dark eyes on him every few seconds.

"I'm tired, not dying," Diego grumbled.

"It is not done yet," Groosh responded enigmatically.

"Yes, the Resh. We still have to get out of the system."

Groosh didn't say anything. That troubled Diego, as the Turengens were talkative creatures. The control room door swished open, and Diego wasn't surprised to see all of the commanders, including the rescued high commanders.

Ziron motioned him over. Diego tried to stand up as straight as he could. "Reporting as ordered, Commander Ziron!"

"Sub-Commander Third Class Diego," Ziron began. "You have done well leading the force to repel the invaders."

"Thank you, sir." Then Ziron's words repeated themselves in the young man's mind. Suddenly he realized that he was gaping at the commander. He snapped his jaw shut. "Sub-Commander, sir?"

"It is fitting for one who has exhibited courage and resourcefulness against the enemy. It is not much in return for what you are going to be asked next."

Diego stood straighter. "I am yours to command, Commander Ziron."

A slight smile touched the commander's mouth. "Yes.

You will command a diversionary shuttle. Pilot Prengi will accompany you, as will several Turengen."

"Yes, sir!" Diego hesitated, and then asked, "Marix, may I ask what I will be doing with the shuttle?"

"Of course. We have been sending messages that the commanders will be evacuating by the fastest available escape shuttle. You will be taking the high commander's shuttle. His ship, The Dragon Claw, is waiting at the following coordinates." Ziron motioned him over to the map table, where a holographic representation of the Koressian solar system appeared. Diego was shown the course he would need to take to get to the high commander's mothership outside of the solar system. He knew the chances of making it were slim, especially when he saw the enemy ships assembling around Koress. He felt someone's presence at his elbow.

It was Prengi. The pilot studied the map. He kept his thoughts to himself.

"Do you think they will believe the shuttle has the commanders?" Diego asked.

"I think so, Diego. They have their own intelligence about the damage aboard my ship. Your use of the concussion armaments to get into the engine room plays into this scenario as well." Ziron stood up straight. His reptilian eyes bored into Diego's. "You and I both know this is most likely a suicide mission. I also know you came into my service unwillingly, and owe nothing to the Seressin rulership."

"I am loyal to you, Lord Ziron. We will make it." Diego was a bit dismayed to hear his voice crack slightly.

If Ziron noticed, he didn't indicate it. "I know you will. I chose wisely. You had better leave quickly before they have time to bring their ships closer."

"Yes, Marix."

He, Prengi, and Groosh left the bridge and headed directly toward the shuttle bay, where the high commander's shuttle sat ready. Rreengrol was standing at the hatch.

"Here to send us off on our one-way trip?" Prengi queried.

"No, I am here to help you get out of this mess." Rreengrol gave a toothy grin. "There are two weaponry consoles."

"There are a half dozen Turengen, too," Diego retorted.

Rreengrol shrugged. "I still think it will show up better on their instruments if there were three 'commanders' on board."

"Huh?" Diego said.

"We're not the same mass as the Seressin commanders, but we're closer than the Turengens."

"Quit yakking and get on board," Prengi ordered.

They got. Diego sealed the hatch while Prengi did a hasty pre-flight. The pilot had the shuttle in the air and winging out of the launch bay before Diego had fully strapped himself in. He picked himself off the deck and slid back into the extra weaponry station seat next to Rreengrol. The ship had rotated so that the launch bay was facing open space. That didn't stop a Resh ship from trying to cut them off. Groosh and Rreengrol fired at the same time, lasers that raked the bottom of the enemy craft. Apparently they had not expected such quick action from the shuttle. Diego could see the white-hot metal as the ship rolled away. Groosh gave them a parting shot. So did the commander's ship. They were both good. The enemy vessel blossomed into a silent fireball that expanded almost to their jet port before falling back on itself. Debris pinged against the shielded hull.

"Good shooting," Prengi crowed. "Now let's see if the rest of the Resh fleet is this easy to take care of."

Diego made no comment. He stayed focused on the monitor, noting that several spacecraft were following them.

"Crab guts!" Groosh cursed.

Diego widened his view of the system and saw what the Turengen was upset about. A large war cruiser loomed from behind the next planet in the Koress system. It was monstrous! It was almost as large as the moon that orbited the gas giant.

"What do we do now, Commander?" Prengi asked, his voice subdued.

"Do an evasive and let's see how he responds," Diego said after a moment's thought.

"Yes, sir," Prengi responded.

"Keep a sharp eye on what's behind us. I doubt one ship's loss is going to deter our followers that much. Especially if they think we are high commanders and commanders."

"Take the command chair," Rreengrol suggested. "I think you can see more of what's going on there. The Turengen and I can handle the weapons systems."

As much as Diego hated leaving the console, he knew the otter-men had quicker reflexes than he did, and Rreengrol was more experienced.

It felt weird sitting in the large chair. He was a squire. At the very least, he was the lowest of the low in the hierarchy of commanders. Still, the array of systems that showed as he sat down in the chair astonished him. Every angle of the little ship was displayed, inside and out. He could see what was behind them, in front, and on each side. There was a read-out of their fuel, the defensive shields, offensive weaponry, all of it. Diego knew Commander Ziron didn't have all of this in his personal shuttle. It made his hopes for survival rise a little bit.

Prengi changed course without warning, almost dumping Diego from the chair. To his surprise safety straps circled his lap and chest and snapped him in. He watched the monitor showing the reaction of the various ships. About half of the fleet that had been harassing Commander Ziron's ship was following them. The large ship ahead changed course slightly, but it was enough to intercept them on their present course. Prengi cut back and then in another direction. Again the large ship altered slightly.

"He's anticipating," Diego muttered. He remembered when wolves or cougars would attack the herds. They had different strategies for different animals. Cattle were slow—they could worry them. Horses were faster—they had to work in concert to cull out a likely meal. The one ship was ponderous, but the others were faster. There were three other ships accompanying the larger battle cruiser. Sometimes even the protection of a corral wasn't enough to keep a hungry predator or pack of predators away. What did the horses do when attacked?

Prengi continued changing course. They were slowly being herded back toward Ziron's ship.

"Okay, Leader, what do we do now?" Rreengrol asked from the weaponry console. His eyes were a deeper amber. He knew what a tight spot they were in. "No asteroids to play around in."

Then something occurred to Diego, something he had learned from Anaar. "Fly closer to that gas giant," he ordered.

Rreengrol growled in surprise.

Prengi choked. "You mean the planet with the giant spaceship nearby waiting to take us?"

"When you are close enough, blast the moon." Diego turned to the Turengen. "We have enough fire power to break it up?"

"Which one?" Groosh asked. "The little one? More than enough."

Diego considered. "Which one would cause that star cruiser the most problems?"

Prengi snickered, while Rreengrol purred in anticipation. Groosh's eyes sparkled. "The big one."

"Can we do it?"

"I'll figure out a way!" Groosh declared.

Prengi continued to pilot an evasive course toward the outer edges of the solar system. He changed their velocity, even while he changed their course. It kept the smaller ships behind them scrambling to keep up, but the ship ahead angled toward them with aggravating ease. Groosh's stubby little fingers flew over the computer screen. The huge cruiser continued to grow larger in their monitors, approaching the gas giant on a different trajectory.

"We have to get within their firing range to make our trick work," Groosh announced.

"I know." Diego studied the screens that flashed on the command chair. Commander Ziron's ship was arrowing out of the system in a different direction, but they were not out of danger either. The shuttle had to draw more attention, but how? Then he remembered something else from his days on the hacienda. Birds that fooled their prey by acting as though they had broken wings. How could they pretend to be disabled without actually being captured; or worse, destroyed? The information on his screens didn't help him any. "We need to make them believe we are disabled so we can drift close enough without them firing on us or using their tractor beams."

Rreengrol growled again. "That will only happen if they think they have scored a hit on us."

Diego tapped on the arm rest of the command chair, thinking. He wished he was more familiar with the way these ships operated. "I am showing my ignorance, but I'm not going to pretend I know what I'm doing. Is there any way to be aware when they are going to fire at us?"

A Turengen named Mruf dashed over to Diego. "Here, Commander." He pointed at a read-out screen to Diego's left. "Numbers go up, we know they are powering up. This one...." Mruf pointed to another small screen below it. "Shows when shields are down for weapon's firing."

"And the shields have to be turned off to fire."

"No one likes weapon bursts coming back at you," Groosh chittered.

Diego did some quick figuring. "If I ask something impossible, let me know, but this is what I propose. Keep speed, but make it look like we are losing control. Might make their response less damaging."

"Better keep your safety harnesses on, then," Prengi commented.

The ship began spinning. It was a little disconcerting looking at the outside monitors, but the ship's gravity controls helped keep equilibrium inside. That might soon change.

"How much do you think they can read from us?"

"Weapons, same thing we can read from them," Rreengrol answered. "I believe we are shielded from intrusion in any other regard. This is a pretty secure ship. High commanders don't like eavesdroppers."

One thing in our favor, Diego thought.

Prengi continued his wild gyrating toward the gas giant. Diego continued watching the monitors. The numbers surged. "They're getting ready to fire."

"Ready for extra power to the front defensive shields," Rreengrol responded with a hiss.

"Wait until the last possible second, in case they can read that." Diego's eyes were riveted on the screens. The weapon's monitor spiked. "They're firing!"

"Shields up, maximum!"

Prengi had been monitoring the other ship's signatures, and slightly rolled away from the energy torpedo that lanced toward them.

"Not too much," Diego ordered. "Want them to think we've been disabled."

"As long as we don't fry," Prengi muttered.

It was close enough. The shuttle shuddered and gyrated into a rough opposite spin. Prengi did nothing to stop it. "This look disabled enough?"

Diego gulped, willing his queasy stomach to behave. "Uh, yes. Should fool them." He studied the read-outs. "And you have us in position to blast that moon, too."

"Of course. Should be in range in…5.23 meka-drons."

Diego translated in his head. A few more minutes would tell if their ploy had been successful or not. Whether they'd be dead or not. He thought of Miguel and his South American bolas, and then about his classes detailing all the nuances of space travel. "Can we use the gas giant's gravity to gain more momentum when we're ready to destroy the moon? Swing around it after we fire on the moon?"

"Sure, but we might have a better chance of using that trick if our torpedo doesn't go off on impact," Rreengrol replied. "We'll be timing it close, because too much of a delay will tip off the Resh."

"If we don't try, we might as well fly into the moon and not worry about torpedoes," Diego returned.

"We're going to singe our tails, but I think we might be able to do it." The new sub-commander tried to do some quick math in his head, but Prengi was quicker. "Got it. Adding thrust now. Be ready with weapons."

"I'm ready," growled Rreengrol. "Let's do this!"

Diego felt the push of the extra thrust. He fought it, leaning forward so he could continue to watch all the monitors. The Resh ship was now behind the giant planet, difficult for their sensors to get the information. He knew it was approaching from the other side of the planet, hoping to surprise them — or hoping they'd turn and run. They'd practically be flying down the warship's gullet. There was a slight shift as Prengi and his Turengren crew made an adjustment, then another. The monitor made it appear that they were moving at snail speed, but Diego knew that wasn't so. He still wished this experiment was over with. Being responsible for even the few lives in this small cruiser wasn't to his liking.

"We will have two meka-drons to get away. Not sure that will be enough," Rreengrol announced.

"It will have to be enough," Diego replied.

"Our escape thrust will have to be more than the safe limits of gravity," Prengi added.

"Will you be able to maintain consciousness?"

"I believe so, Commander."

"Let's do it!" Diego knew it was time.

"Lowering shields and firing," Rreengrol called out.

"Thrusssssttt." Prengi hit the thrusters so hard that his announcement came out in a stream.

Diego was amazed at how precise his team was. All three activities were done in the same second. As the little ship shot away from the gas giant, he didn't try to fight the pull of gravity. Diego's body ground against the cushion so hard he felt the hard back of the chair digging into his spine. His body felt massive; he couldn't breathe.

"Det'nation two tola-drons, one tola…." Rreengrol hissed. "Theenk we…."

A blast hit the ship, sirens blared, and heat engulfed the cabin in an instant. The lights flickered and then went out; only the amber emergency lights remained on. The ship felt like a stone careening down a hill; bouncing, rolling, tossing up, and banging back against a hard ground. Diego's head felt like a ball. The emergency lights flickered, but they remained on. Sparks flew from Prengi's console. The pilot managed to reach forward and press a button. Blue steam hissed from above the console, and the sparks were extinguished. Whether it was the blast or the ship's thrust, they were still moving forward at incredible speed.

Another shock wave hit them, and Diego lost all awareness.

Chapter Twenty-Four

He awoke to cries and moans, realizing that some of those moans were coming from him. Something thick wrapped around his legs and torso, and cushioned his head. It didn't cushion the pounding inside, though. Thick darkness enveloped the cabin. Diego moved his arm and felt a quick stab of pain from his earlier injury. The wrappings fell away from his body, although the safety straps were still secure. "Rreengrol! Prengi!" he called. His answer was a hiss and a soft groan.

Diego fumbled with the straps, and they came loose. He floated out of the chair. His stomach lurched, but he ignored it as he worked to navigate around the cabin. Diego called his friends again, adding "Report!" Grabbing the back of the command chair, he propelled himself toward the groaning. His body banged into a console, and he reached for some kind of handhold. That put him in a slow spin. Diego relaxed, and his momentum slowed. He bumped against something soft and warm. Prengi? Trying to feel his shipmate without gravity was difficult, but Diego found the back of a chair and hung on with one hand. "Prengi."

Another moan answered. Short clawed fingers grabbed his sleeve. "Commander?" Prengi whispered.

"Right now we're all equal. So just call me Diego."

"Diego, need to get…online."

"We need to get some power so we can see what we're doing to get back online."

"Not sure I can do it."

"Yes, you can. What can I do to help?"

A soft light flashed from the other side of the cabin, hitting him in the eyes. Diego couldn't tell who was behind it until a voice called his name. "Rreengrol," he answered. "Can you flash that somewhere else? Like maybe around the cabin to see if anyone needs medical assistance."

"Of course, Commander. I wanted to see how you were first," the feline warrior hissed.

"I am fine. How are you, my friend?" Diego asked, his tone softened. "And as I told Prengi, we are all equals here."

"Rattled my brain a bit. Think I broke my leg."

"We need to take care of injuries," Diego began.

"No, we need to get this ship back in some kind of service," Rreengrol replied. "I'm surprised the Resh cruiser didn't finish what the moon began."

"Maybe the moon finished the cruiser," Prengi suggested with a whistling snort.

"It would be nice to have that kind of luck," Rreengrol muttered. His light flickered throughout the cabin. Mruf was huddled under the weapon's console, unmoving. Groosh was floating limply toward what normally would be the ceiling.

Diego couldn't see any of the other Turengen. Something splatted against his cheek, and he rubbed it off. Squinting to see what it was in the dim light, he realized it had to be blood. Wiping it on his jumpsuit, Diego pushed himself across the room to Rreengrol. The cat-man's leg was broken cleanly, halfway between the foot and knee. The amber eyes registered pain, but his friend was smiling.

"A good win is one you can walk, or in our case, float away from."

"That's fine, but I wish we could find out what's going on."

"Maybe there is a way to," Prengi offered, floating over to the pair. "Let me check the life support first."

"Yes, and I'll take care of our navigator," Diego replied.

"I'll be okay. We need to...."

"We need to take care of injuries first. And get life support up and running," Diego admonished his friend. He floated to the medical locker and grabbed a kit as it drifted out of the cabinet. Several cans followed. Diego snagged the ones he needed, stuffed them in his jumpsuit, and floated back to Rreengrol. The Grrlock was trying to maneuver under the console. "Lay still...and that's an order."

Rreengrol sighed and did as he was told. It never ceased to amaze Diego how easy it was to doctor an injury among the stars. Of course, it was easier to destroy life out here, too. He thumbed the button of the internal diagnosing device and ran it over Rreengrol's leg. As suspected, the leg was broken. Diego applied the local anesthetic. Another device told him how to set the leg. He followed the directions. The only thing similar to what he was used to back on Earth was the action that would straighten the bones. Rreengrol's reaction to his first aid was a loud hiss and a quick growl. With a push of a button, the next container sprayed out a thick liquid that covered his friend's leg and hardened almost instantaneously.

Diego sat back and gazed at Rreengrol's face. The Grrlock appeared more comfortable. The first aid containers began floating away. Rreengrol grabbed one while Diego caught the others, stuffing them into a bag.

"You'd better check the others," Rreengrol suggested. "I can work on the navigational equipment in zero gravity without trouble."

Diego nodded and pushed himself away from the console. Groosh was nearby, and he checked the little alien first. The same diagnostic tool that told him his friend had a broken leg informed him the Turengen was dead. Diego crossed himself, praying that the otter-man was safely in whatever hereafter he believed in. "Thank you, my friend. I could not have asked for a better compadre," he murmured. He told Prengi and Rreengrol.

A check of the others showed various bumps, bruises, and another broken bone, but all the rest were alive. One by one, Diego floated them to the nearest chairs and strapped them in. One of the containers in the first aide locker contained a stimulant, and he used it to rouse the others. He needed all of his remaining crew to try and get the shuttle back into working order.

Lights came back on, and several consoles whirred back into life. "Good job, Prengi!"

Several of the Turengen whistled in pain as they woke up, but they unstrapped themselves and pushed off toward their duty stations.

"You might want to come see this, Commander," Rreengrol called.

The tone of his friend's voice kept him from admonishing his formality. He floated over.

"I have limited ability to observe what's outside, but thought you'd like to see this."

Diego gazed into the scanner. At first, he wasn't sure what he was looking for, but as several large objects floated within the scanner's view, he realized he was looking at the remains of a spaceship. The cruiser!

"You did it, Diego," Rreengrol hissed.

"We did it. All of us." Diego continued studying their surroundings. "I don't see any other ships."

"Scanner can't detect that far. I still have to get our other monitors online."

"We've got company! I am picking up sounds of a ship approaching," Prengi announced.

"Can you tell whose it is?" Diego asked.

"No, Commander."

Diego growled, grinding his teeth in frustration. Of course, it had been a long shot that they would succeed in not only living, but getting away as well. They couldn't fight, and they couldn't run. "Cut off the systems."

"Play dead?" Rreengrol asked.

"Really can't do anything else. Unless someone has another idea. I'd be open to any suggestions."

"They can still detect life forms. So we could play dead, but I want to try to surprise them when they come on board," Rreengrol suggested.

"Yes, at least we will go out with honor," Diego concurred. "Let's see what's left in the arms lockers, and then get into your enviro-suits."

A few moments later, the cabin was again pitch dark. The soft chirp of the one or two working consoles was silent. All Diego could hear was the beating of his own heart inside the space suit. The clunk of metal against the hull and the jerk of their shuttle as it was attached to a larger ship made him jump. He felt a partial return of gravity, and braced as he hit the floor. His heart thudded louder, but he forced his breathing to calm. Diego tightened his grip on his laser pistol. Rreengrol waited on the other side of the command chair, a flash rifle held easily in his hands.

There were more metal against metal sounds, and the whoosh of the outer airlock opening. At least they were kind enough not to cut open the hull.

The inner hatch opened. A beam of light played across the deck and consoles. Rreengrol started to move, but Diego motioned him still. He wanted to be sure they were attacking Koress guardsmen. Enviro-suited beings entered, three together. *Not smart*, Diego thought. He couldn't tell if they were friend or foe. He raised his weapon, but they fired some kind of palm weapon, spraying the room in bright light which sent him into darkness....

***

Diego woke to warmth, light, and familiar voices speaking the Seressin language. He opened his eyes to the ceiling of a med bay; a very large one. It was bigger than the one he had been sent to most recently. It even smelled different.

"The young sub-commander has awakened, Lord Ziron."

Commander Ziron? Diego tried to sit up, but his body betrayed him. He could barely move his hand, much less anything else.

Ziron stood beside the bed, a broad grin on his face. "Despite what I witnessed in the early days of your training, there was something that told me you were leader material."

"Sir? How, uh, what happened, sir?"

"I am told that it was your idea to explode the Koress gas planet moon."

"Yes, sir."

Ziron chuckled. "It also set half of the planet on fire, destroyed the two nearest battle cruisers, and blew the shuttle halfway out of the Koress system."

"How did we survive?"

"Your navigator had the foresight to raise protective shields aft."

Still, Diego thought, *it was scant protection from the power of the explosion we set off.*

As if perceiving his thoughts, Ziron continued. "It so happened that one of those cruisers was between you and the main force of the destruction. Its explosion threw the shuttle farther out of the solar system, as well as protected your ship." He shrugged. "I would say cosmic luck had a great deal to do with it, as well. By all rights, every one of you should have been dead."

Then everything clicked into place. His commander had survived. The commander's ship had escaped. "Sir, you are all right!" he exclaimed, immediately realizing what an inane thing he had said.

Ziron laughed, his sharp teeth clacking his intense

pleasure. "Of course. How else could it be? And I was not about to leave any of my brave sub-commanders behind. Even if it might have only been their bodies I recovered."

"Sub-commanders?" Diego asked still groggy.

"You all have been promoted within your spheres of occupation."

Diego drew in a quavering breath. "Then I am no longer a slave? Sir?"'

Ziron shook his head. "Your bravery gave you your freedom back on the plains of Koress. But, no, you are officially a citizen of the Seressin Empire."

***

Diego could scarcely believe it several weeks later when an attendant came into his quarters on the Seressin home world with the uniform of a sub-commander of the second rank. His fingers brushed the raised stitching of the crossed dragon swords on each shoulder circled in metallic thread. The attendant bowed and held his hands out to help him on with the uniform jacket.

"No, thank you, I want to put it on myself." He saw the hurt look on the slave's face and added, "It has nothing to do with the quality of your service. It's just that it wasn't that long ago that I was a slave. I want to feel this transition totally on my own." He gazed into the tall, slender-limbed Filosian's red eyes for understanding.

"It isss good to haf sssomething to hope for."

"Yes, it is." Diego drew on the uniform and let the lizard-like man buckle on his ceremonial sword belt and the smaller weapon's belt. "Thank you."

"Go with honor; go with peassse," the alien intoned.

"With luck...."

"No luck. With bravery and honor, my lord," the Filosian added.

Diego nodded as he left the cabin and headed to the assembly of high commanders in the great hall of heroes.

Who would have thought? Diego wondered as he passed between the rows of guards standing on each side of the wide walkway. Above him, the ceilings were tall enough to touch the sky, larger than any cathedral his mother had described from her home in Spain. He thought of his mother. She would be proud of all he had accomplished. Diego felt that even Father would be impressed. He had, after all, told Diego he would have to go out and make a life for himself. And Miguel.... Diego felt the spirit of his vaquero mentor watching him, and knew his friend was pleased.

Behind him, also in resplendent sub-commander uniforms, marched Rreengrol, limping slightly, Prengi, and a fairly large contingent of Turengen. Diego could hear the Turengen half-purring, half-chittering under their breath in pride for their whole family, for all of them had been given their freedom as well as citizenship in the Empire. Leading the way was Lurin, grumbling under his breath at the chafing uniform of his rank.

Jangling Seressin fanfare brought his mind back to the group of high commanders waiting ahead of them, the supreme commander of all the Seressin Empire in the center of the group. Diego felt a pang at the knowledge he most likely wouldn't be riding across the wide hills of his native Alta California ever again. Then he realized he would be riding among the stars to places unimaginable a scant year ago.

Who would have thought?

About the Author

Susan Kite was born in Indiana, but because her father was in the Army, she moved extensively during her growing up years. The post library was the first place she found after a move, avidly reading fantasy, science fiction, and many other genres. In her teens, she dabbled in writing, creating stories based on characters from her favorite TV shows. With college and marriage, writing was mostly put on hold.

That changed more than twenty years ago when the writing bug bit again. For a decade, fan fiction was the main focus, but this provided practice and helped develop skills needed to write original works. A visit to the Mission San Luis Rey in California in 2001 and subsequent research became the catalyst to write her first novel, *My House of Dreams*. *The Mendel Experiment*, and its sequels, *Blue Fire, and Power Stone of Alogol*, were published by World Castle.

The author earned her Bachelor's degree in secondary English and followed that up with a Master's degree in Instructional Media at Utah State University. She worked in public school libraries for 35 years, most recently in Chattanooga, Tennessee. Now retired, Ms. Kite lives in Oklahoma City. She has been married to the love of her life, Daniel, for over 40 years. They have two children and seven grandchildren and are owned by an opinionated chiweenie-terrier.

Made in the USA
Middletown, DE
12 June 2020

96549536R00135